CHATTERBONE

Megan Guilliams

Any and all characters are a work of fiction and belong to the author. Any use of plot, characters, and direct plagiarism will be subject to copyright infringement.

Copyright © 2024 by Megan Guilliams
All rights reserved.

ISB: 9798333401472

10 9 8 7 6 5 4 3 2 1

All rights reserved. No part of this publication may be reproduced, distributed, or transmitted in any form or by any means, including photocopying, recording, or other electronic or mechanical methods, without the prior written permission of the publisher, except in the case of brief quotations embodied in critical reviews and certain other noncommercial uses permitted by copyright law.

Printed in the United States of America

Original Cover
Design By Kasey Hill

Chapter One
I Didn't Mean for This to Happen.

I walked up to the convenience store with sweaty palms. I knew it was five minutes before close, but I didn't care. Label me as one of 'those' guys, do it! I don't care. After the day I've had it didn't matter anyway. I'm sure the others had called me worse behind closed doors. My name is Beatrice Bones. Yes, that's my real name, and no, I'm not some kind of goth wannabe. Usually, during the daylight hours, you'd find me behind a computer screen with my thick glasses falling off my nose. I'm a geek, but usually, that's all I am. My best friend, Smita Chatter, does most of the leg work... Oh, I guess I didn't tell you the story yet... You know... About who we are and what we do. I don't have a lot of time right now, what with the store closing and all, but you can hang around, that is, if you can keep up.

Pushing the door open, I walked through the dimly lit store. The lady up front didn't bother looking up from her phone to notice how

5

disheveled I was. Thank goodness for small favors.

"Excuse me," I said as I cleared my throat awkwardly. "Where are your cleaning supplies?" Popping her gum, the lady behind the counter pointed to the store's back corner before scrolling down on her shining screen.

"Thanks," I muttered.

As I walked down the aisle towards the back of the store, I could hear the squishing of my shoes. It had rained earlier in the day, but I didn't have to look down to know what was making; that noise was no water. Grimacing, I closed my eyes as I turned the corner.

"Wow there, I almost mowed you down." The boy's voice made me open my eyes quickly. I stumbled back, but he grabbed my hand to steady me. The guy couldn't have been more than twenty. He was tall and lanky with shoulder-length black hair he had tied loosely behind him. He had a thin, crooked smile painted across his face and a look in his eye that said he could be trouble. He had on a white work shirt and was pushing a broom. His nametag said Tom, but he looked much more exotic. "Where's the fire?" Tom asked with a sniff.

"No fire... Just a mess." I stammered as I looked over the boy's shoulder. The cleaning supplies were right behind him, but he looked like he didn't intend to move out of the way. Leaning against the shelf between myself and my intended purpose, Tom smirked even harder and shrugged his shoulders.

"You sure are making a mess of things, " he muttered, his nose wrinkling slightly.

"What do you mean?" I snapped as I stepped back a bit. For some reason, I didn't want to be within arm's reach of the thin man in the hallway. Pointing down, Tom lifted an eyebrow and then glanced into my eyes.

"Whatever you stepped into, it's following you around the store, and I can't leave until I mop all that shit up. You know you really should have more respect for your blue-collar workers."

"Yeah, well, if you move, I'll get what I came for and leave." I could feel my cheeks getting hotter as the smart comment left my lips. Normally, I would have never spoken to another person that way, but tonight, I just didn't have the patience. Smiling, Tom bowed sarcastically as he waved me down the walkway. Sniffing the air as I passed, he looked at the green goop that covered the tops and soles of my brand-new white high-tops.

"What DID you step in anyway?" The boy asked as he ran his broom over the puddle I had created. Sighing, I bent down and read the labels on the gallon jugs of cleaner on the bottom shelf.

"Trust me, Tom, if I told you, I'd have to kill you."

I didn't choose the cryptid life; the cryptid life chose me... Or maybe I did; I don't really know anymore. With each passing day, the line between what I knew as reality and fairytale stories blurred. I feel like Smita, and I walk a thin line between sane and insane. It can be rather taxing on the nerves. Unlike myself, my best friend Smita strives in an environment like this one. She's fast and witty, and to be honest, she had the longest, prettiest curly hair I had ever laid eyes on. If given half the chance, I believe Smita would have died doing what she loves... All her own stunts.

We met a few years ago. I had an apartment in the city with an extra room, and she had a trust fund with enough money to keep us comfortable. As a struggling college student, I jumped at the chance to have a roommate who was barely home and didn't eat all my yogurt, and for a while, things were really good... That was until I found out what she did for a living. Of course, I reacted the way you would think a sane person would. I laughed it off. I thought she was trying to prank me. I lived in my safe little daytime world and wanted to keep it that way. Cryptids didn't exist... Did they?

Reaching down, I picked up a bottle of blue cleaner and a gallon of bleach. Brushing past the man with the broom, I shoved a couple of sponges into my pocket for good measure.

"Hey... I hope you're not going to mix those together." Tom called as he skipped a few times, attempting to keep up with me.

"What if I am? Are you the dust bunny police or that bald dude on the cover of those weird white brushes?" Snorting, Tom shrugged his shoulders and stopped behind me as I put the products down on the counter. Pulling the sponges out of my pocket, I took a twenty-dollar-bill and slammed it on the counter. The cashier looked up from her phone and popped her gum, rolling her eyes at how dramatic I was being.

"You know, we closed like ten minutes ago." She said with a slow southern drawl. I couldn't tell if she was just slow or if she had popped a muscle relaxer while I was in the back of the store.

"Yeah," I muttered. "I appreciate you staying open a little longer." As the woman rang up my things, Tom leaned into my ear, smelling my hair in a creepy sort of way, and then whispered something into my ear I never would have imagined.

"Mustard gas," Snapping around, I pulled away from the custodian. I must have had a shocked expression because Tom couldn't stifle his giddiness.

"Excuse me?" I asked. This time, it was my turn to pull on the words, emphasizing my exasperation with the man.

"If you mix those, you're going to make mustard gas. I couldn't just let you leave here without that little tidbit of knowledge." Reaching over my shoulder, the man turned the blue bottle around and pointed to the main ingredients. "See? Ammonia."

"I would have figured it out," I replied. I didn't bother looking over my shoulder. I knew his smirk was large, and I was in the mood to slap someone. The lady handed me my receipt and my change, and I grabbed the bags, making my way out into the parking lot.

"Hey! Wait!" Tom called as he bounded out the door behind me. "I didn't even catch your name." I could hear the man's black no-slips tapping across the parking lot and stopped halfway to turn and face him. Blowing a piece of my frizzy black hair away from my eyes, I groaned at the night sky.

"Do you do this to all your customers?" I asked with irritation. Dropping the sticky broom between us, the man shrugged and smiled slyly once more.

"It's just that Delilah... You know the girl at the cash register?"

"Oh, was that her name?" I asked. I couldn't tell if Tom was picking up on my sarcasm, but it didn't divert him from his new mission. Fumbling with the two-gallon bottles in my hands, I didn't wait for him to continue his story. I had more pressing things to attend to at the moment.

"At least let me help you with those bottles." Tom insisted. Jumping over the broom, he wedged himself between me and the van that had begun to shake as something inside fought to get out. If Tom had noticed, he wasn't letting it bother him.

"Look, I'm sure your girlfriend would like to get out of here at some point tonight. Why don't you go back inside and finish up? I got it from here... Okay." Shaking his head, Tom put a finger in the air and waggled it a little before turning around. By then, the van had stopped shaking, but I could feel my heart pounding a mile a minute as the man put a hand on the van's handles.

"The least I can do is open the door for you." Dropping the bottles, I ran towards Tom, but it was too late by then. A green light flashed as it knocked us both to the ground. One of the van doors swung open, slamming against the side of the vehicle and the other made a weird sort of groaning noise before falling off our ride completely. I could hear Smita inside the van cursing at us in Arabic.

"What the hell are you thinking? I told you to open the door carefully; you blew right through the last of our sulfur."

"Oh, oh man, what's that smell... It's like rotten eggs and... dog breath." Sitting up, Tom covered his nose with the crook of his arm, looking back at me in disgust. I was lying flat on my back in a puddle. I could feel the dirty street water soaking through my jeans and into my underwear. Yes, I had to admit, it was the perfect ending to a perfect day. Scrambling from the van, Smita jumped over Tom's legs and knelt beside me while I stared at the starless night, contemplating life.

"Birdie, are you alright?" Smita asked as she brushed the wild hair from my face. "Don't worry, we'll get the Squonk another day." Reaching up, I took my friend's hand and looked her in the eye.

"Do you think we'll be able to outwit it again? The mobile unit smells like farts and foes."

"What the hell are you two talking about?" Tom asked as he got to his feet. "What exploded from the back of your van?" Pressing her lips together, Smita pulled me to my feet and ushered me into the passenger seat of our car. She shut the door behind me, but I managed to roll the window down enough to hear their conversation.

"So... Tom, what were you doing following my friend out into the parking lot in the first place?" Smita asked as she flicked the man's nametag. Flaring his nostrils, Tom crossed his arms and shifted his weight onto his left foot. He was a good six inches taller than Smita, but it didn't stop her from commanding respect. It was another thing she had in spades that I lacked entirely.

"I thought she might need a little help getting to her car. It's late, and there are weirdos out here."

13

"Yeah," Smita said with a snort. "I can see that." Walking away from the van, the woman flipped her cinnamon-colored hair over her shoulder and picked up the forgotten cleaning supplies. "Maybe you should go clock out and get some rest, Tom. I believe your work here is done."

"Yeah... Maybe." Tom said, a little defeated. Taking a few steps toward the store, he picked up the broom and gave it a good shake, dipping the green goo into my forgotten puddle. The scent of rotten produce filled the air, permeating the already horrendous scent of sulfur and Squonk tears. Seconds later, Smita stopped in her tracks. Grabbing Tom by his sleeve, she looked over at him with horror.

"Scratch that. You need to get into the van... NOW."

"Why?" Tom asked, a little amused, but stopped smirking when he heard the noise that had entertained Smita's ears first.

"What is that?" I called from the crack in the window. "It sounds like..."

"Crying," Smita called back. "It's the Squonk. It smells our lure." Squinting her eyes, Smita looked across the parking lot. She could barely make out the pig-like creature. It had already begun to burrow underground. Pulling Tom towards the van, Smita threw him into the back with surprising force. Tom's broom fell from his grasp, landing by the bumper with a clang.

"What are you doing?" He yelled, struggling to regain his footing.

"Saving your ass!" She called back. Slamming the door still attached to the van, Smita rushed towards the driver's side, barely missing the hole that had formed by the back tire. Suddenly, a long, misshapen nose emerged, pulling the broom down into the abyss.

"Don't touch the tears!" I screamed back as Smita kickstarted the engine, squealing tires and leaving the monster in the dust.

Ignoring the red light on Parks Ave, Smita pushed the pedal to the floor and drifted through the parking garage at the end of the street.

"What the hell was that!" Tom screamed as he rolled around in the back.

"I thought I told you. Didn't we tell him?" Smita asked. She seemed quite unphased by the attack, but I could still feel my heart pounding against my chest. "Oh, is he hard of hearing?" She asked as she glanced over in my direction. Fixing the rearview mirror, Smita looked into the van's bed and smiled as politely as she knew how. "WE WERE TRYING TO CAPTURE A

SQUONK. IT DIDN'T GO SO WELL BECAUSE IT STARTED CRYING. I SENT BIRDIE IN TO GET A FEW THINGS, BUT YOU LET IT ESCAPE, AND NOW IT'S MAD." Touching my friend on the shoulder, I stifled a giggle.

"He's not hard of hearing. I think he's just scared." Looking down at his hands, Tom grimaced and then scooted back against the corner as far away from the open door as possible.

"So, I'm stuck in a van with two crazy women, covered in... What? Some pig's postnasal drip?" Reaching back, Smita smacked the back of Tom's head with an open palm.

"I told you not to touch that." Shifting the car into park, Smita drifted into an empty parking spot and pulled the keys out of the ignition. "Come on, we don't have a lot of time."

"A lot of time before what?" Tom asked as he scooted closer to the opening in the back of the van.

"Before she wakes up."

Chapter Two
Well, now you've gone and done it.

About three years ago, Smita Chatter stepped onto my welcome mat. I had put the 'Roommate Wanted' sign on the wall of my Elite Fitness Center women's locker room in hopes of weeding out the crazies. Making friends here in the big city was hard, and I certainly didn't want to put an ad up on one of those online sites.

Smita rang the doorbell and gave me a heartwarming smile and before I knew what was happening, I gave her a paper to sign for our cohabitation. Things went well for a while. I believe we were almost a year in when it all fell apart. It had to be three in the morning when I was jarred from my sleep. The front door to my apartment slammed, and I could hear pacing from the other room. Rubbing my eyes, I padded across the carpeted floor and opened the door. Smita was walking the living room length with her hand on her chin. I could tell that she was in deep thought, but I couldn't understand the severity of the situation for the life of me.

"Smita, it's three in the morning. Why don't you go to bed? Things always seem more dire than they really are when your sleep deprived." Laughing a little to herself, the woman stopped pacing and glanced at me with a wild look.

"It's funny you should say that because I don't know if I could think of a situation more dire than this one." Crossing her arms, the woman began to tap her foot and then looked at the floor with trepidation. Lowering my eyebrow, I could see something hidden just under her shirt sleeve. It glimmered in the overhead, soaking through Smita's cotton clothes.

"Did you hurt yourself at work? Are you bleeding?" Rushing to the woman's side, I tried to examine her wound, but Smita pulled away, babying the arm and guarding its exposure with her life.

"Ugh! I didn't want to tell you like this. I didn't want you to find out so soon."

"What are you talking about?" I asked. Walking past the woman, I ventured into the kitchen ad opened the top cabinet. Turning on the water, I filled a glass and listened through the open door.

"Well, you know I keep weird hours, and I'm vague about what I do."

"Hey, I don't care what your job is as long as you keep paying your rent." I was only half joking. If it weren't for Smita, I would have been out on the street long ago. Now, as I hit my doctorate era, I had been struggling to find the right thesis. I needed something that would blow my professors away. I wanted to stand out and be different... But I had no imagination. So, as you could imagine, holding down a job of my own was just short of impossible.

For the first time ever, I thought I saw the woman shudder as she rocked her arm gently. Whatever she was about to say had become increasingly difficult.

"I'm not a night janitor at the school. Even though my job does take me there, and the local park more than I'd like to admit. You see, I thought I had it all under control. I thought I could keep it together... I was so stupid." Walking over to my friend, I gave her the glass of water. Taking it in her good hand, she laughed and sat it down on the coffee table beside the little couch. "After I manage to spit out what it is, I'm trying to say you might want something a little stronger than water."

19

Wrapping my nightgown tighter, I crossed my arms and frowned.

"What?" I questioned. "What is it? Did you get fired, too?"

"Fired... TOO?" Smita asked, but before she had a chance to say another word, the lights in the little apartment began to flicker. Smoke began to materialize from under the door.

"Oh shit!" I exclaimed, grabbing the woman's arm. "I think the apartment is on fire!" I tried to pull Smita across the apartment floor with all my might, but her feet wouldn't budge. She didn't look frightened or alarmed in any way. It would have been exasperated if I had to describe the woman's expression.

"Calm down. The place isn't on fire." Letting go of Smita, I watched with horror as a shrouded woman began to form between us and the front door.

"What the hell is that!" I exclaimed. "Who the hell is that." I rushed back to my room and slammed the door on my friend and the new intruder. Nothing made sense anymore. Was I still asleep? Was this all a dream? People don't just materialize like that. Covering my heart with my hands, I could feel my heart pounding. My blood was racing through my veins... the first of many times Smita would do that to me.

Leaning against the door, I swallowed hard and tried to calm my breathing. It didn't help that someone was knocking on my door about thirty seconds later. Jumping back and yelping like an injured puppy, I stared down at the floor, waiting for the woman to simply slip through the cracks of my door frame and attack me... But nothing happened.

"Birdie, I need you to come out so I can explain everything. If you can't handle this, I'll understand... But I can't keep things like this between us."

"How did she do that? Slip through the door, I mean. Who's in there with you?" There was a moment of silence while the girls in the living room talked in hushed whispers.

"I have to tell her," Smita whispered.

"She doesn't seem like she's ready for that conversation yet." The woman replied.

"Well, you showed her your hand the moment you smoked your way into the apartment. What else am I going to tell her?"

"I had to make sure you were okay. You were hurt tonight... I could smell it."

"You need to stay away from me. You know what blood does to you." My hands shook, but I knew there wasn't another logical way out.

21

Reaching for the door, I cracked it open and peeked through.

The woman standing before Smita was tall and beautiful with rosy cheeks and strawberry blond hair. She was dressed all in black with some bright gold talisman tied around her neck with a black cord. She could have been anyone on the street that I passed on the daily and would have never known it if it weren't for the black marble eyes and sharp fangs that glistened in the living room lights when she spoke.

"I'm not going to stand here and pretend I don't see your friend eyeballing me from her room." The woman hissed. The sound of her sultry voice sent chills down my spine. Curiosity wanted me to go out and investigate, but the smarter, more refined part of me knew it might be a death trap.

"I didn't tell you to follow me home," Smita said as she backed away from the woman in black. Smiling, she tapped her foot and glanced down at the arm Smita had been hiding.

"If it weren't for me, you wouldn't have gotten hurt. I needed to make sure you weren't gonna go and die on me. I thought we had a deal." Rolling her eyes, Smita began to pace the floor, laughing to herself.

"What do you think you were going to do? Were you going to turn me into one of you?" Wrinkling her nose, Smita shook her head. "I don't think putting 'vampire' on my resume would get me any more gigs."

"Vampire?" I whispered to myself as my eyes widened. Last time I checked, vampires were a thing of fantasy. Some of them glittered, and some turned noodles into worms, but none of them walked with reality... Did they?

"Let me see." The woman barked as she walked towards Smita, who pulled away from her, shaking her head ferociously.

"Are you insane? It'll exacerbate your condition."

"I can control myself long enough to ensure you don't need real medical attention." At this point, my mind was reeling. I didn't know a lot about vampires, but the one thing that stood as a constant no matter how many movies I had watched on the subject was that vampires drank blood... And Smita was bleeding. Pulling myself away from the door, I looked around the room. There had to be something... Anything that would detour the creature in my living room. There was shuffling in the room adjacent to mine, and I knew my time was running out.

"Get off of me, Kasey! I'm fine!"

"No! I need to see what happened." Bursting through the door, I made a beeline towards the glass of water on the table. Picking it up, I drew a cross in its condensation and whispered the Lord's Prayer. I knew I wasn't a priest, but it was the best I could do.

"Take that, you unholy creature of the night!" I screamed. Closing my eyes, I flung the water at the two fighting girls.

"What... What the hell did you do that for?" Smita asked. The struggle had stopped, and the room had gone silent. After a few moments, I ventured to open my eyes. Kasey stood beside Smita, completely untouched by my makeshift holy water, but Smita had caught the whole glass. She was soaked from head to toe, and the wound on her wrist had been aggravated.

"I didn't mean to! I was trying to stop her from biting you."

"Biting her?" Kasey asked as she bobbed a thumb in Smita's direction. Smiling widely, Kasey laughed heartily, tilting her head up at the ceiling. Smita looked much less amused.

"I had it under control." She began as she rolled her sleeves up. Suddenly, Kasey sniffed the air, and her laughter halted. Small blue veins began to emerge just under the fleshy bits under her black eyes. Her nose wrinkled and she grabbed at her stomach, almost as if she were in pain.

"I was wrong." Kasey began, "I thought I would be okay… But I can't control it." I was frozen in place. I wanted to help my friend but didn't know what else to do. Watching in horror, Kasey stumbled forward, grabbing Smita by the shoulder. Opening her mouth, Kasey exposed a pair of pearly whites that would have put a lion's to shame. I watched as Smita closed her eyes, waiting for the worst.

'This was it.' I thought, 'This is how we die.' Somewhere amid it all, I could hear Kasey's stomach. It gurgled and rumbled. Her eyes rolled up into the back of her head, and then she…. Projectile vomited all over the living room floor.

"Oh, for the love of all things holy, will you wrap that up? It smells horrible." Letting go of Smita's shoulder, Kasey doubled over and dry heaved once more before flopping down on the couch.

"I told you you couldn't handle it. Not with your allergy." Rushing to the bathroom, Smita shut the door behind her, leaving me alone with the nocturnal hemophobe. Standing awkwardly beside the woman on the couch, I tried to smile, but I knew it looked more like a grimace.

"So," I began. "How did the two of you meet?"

Chapter Three
Kasey and the Bite

Kasey Tomlin woke up in the hospital on a cold November night. She couldn't remember why she had gone there or how she had even arrived. She was hooked up to all kinds of machines and had a tube down her throat. Closing her eyes once again, she could hear the methodical beeping and booping of all the electronics around her. Even though the lights were dimmed, she couldn't get the tickle of a migraine to go away as the first wave of nausea hit.

Covering her eyes with her arm, Kasey groaned and rolled over on her side. A few moments later, the door to her room opened, and a young man slipped through. He couldn't have been more than forty. He was short and solid wearing a long white coat. In one hand, he held a metal clipboard, and in the other, he had a bag of what looked to be blood.

"I'm sorry to have disturbed your sleep, ma'am. It's just that we haven't seen a case as severe as yours in... Well... Ever." Smiling brightly, the man walked over to the bed and hooked the red bag up, hooking it to Kasey's IV. Taking her arm from her face, Kasey glanced over at the doctor with squinty eyes and clenched her jaw. She could feel the warm ooze as it entered her veins, and it felt like hellfire.

"What is that stuff? What are you doing to me?" the moment Kasey tried to sit up, the man in the white coat jerked back, his eyes wide with fear.

"Don't try anything funny, Kasey. I'm watching you closer now."

"What are you talking about?" Kasey asked again. Something heavy was wrapped around her ankles. As she pulled the stark white sheet from her body, Kasey noticed the thick chains bolted to the bed. "This isn't a hospital... Is it?" She asked. Pushing a button on his earbud, he looked down at the paperwork in his hand and huffed.

"Patient 370013 has lost her memory since we last spoke." Clicking the button on his earbud once more, the man crossed his arms and tapped his foot impatiently. "If you're trying to trick me, Kasey, it won't work. Our primary objective is to get you back on your feet and into testing." Laughing, Kasey shook her head and glanced at the door her captor had come through. Whatever was in the bag had stopped burning, and she had become a little more alert.

"You sound like I'm some military person. My name is Kasey Tomlin, and I run a flower shop off of Orchard." Rolling his eyes, the man clicked the button once more. This time, the sheer irritation in his voice couldn't be masked.

"It looks as if patient 370013 has gone into past life regression. She has no memory of who she used to be. There's nothing else we can do here." Pinching the skin on the bridge of his nose to stave off a headache, the doctor slipped the metal clipboard onto the end of the medical bed and walked towards the door.

"You can't keep me here!" Kasey called. She thought about trying to follow the man in the white coat, but the clinking chains around her ankles said it would have been a bad idea. Grabbing the handle, the man stopped dramatically before opening the door. Looking over his shoulder, he lowered his posture and frowned.

"This is the part of the job I hate. You're just too far gone. That bite did you in."

"I... I don't understand." Kasey screamed.

"Enjoy your meal, 370013; it'll be your last. You're slated for termination at 2100 hours." Kasey couldn't believe what she was hearing.

Everything was happening too fast for her to make heads or tails of it. Closing her eyes, she tried to remember what had happened. Everything was foggy, and in pieces like a puzzle, she had no box to.

Kasey remembered closing the store for the night. The freshly cut flowers had followed her out onto the street, filling the city with hints of orchids and baby's breath. It was an unnaturally warm November, and Kasey wanted to take full advantage of it. Wrapping the brown coat tighter around her arms, she whipped her blonde hair over her shoulder and started her short walk home.

Wracking her brain, she tried as hard as she could to remember anything that was out of the ordinary. She remembered a sound vaguely, in the back of her mind. It sounded like... A baby crying. She remembered fumbling with her keys at the door of her little house, and at some point, she had stopped somewhere to buy fresh fruit. She could hear the crumpling of the paper bag and smell orange rinds. Then, there was nothing. There was blackness all around her. An intense pain in the back of her neck jolted her from her unconsciousness.

Reaching back, Kasey winced as she stuck a finger deep into the hole that still sat open on the base of her neck, just between her shoulder blades. Common sense would have dictated that there was no fusion between the fifth and sixth vertebrae. She should have been paralyzed, but she wasn't. Suddenly, she could remember flashes of crystals, pink, blue, and red, all coming together, creating a halo of light. There was a girl there, fighting a monstrous being. It reminded her of a wolf, but its gray matted fur and inverted leg shape told a different story.

"Rougarou. There was a Rougarou in my house? How do I know what a Rougarou is? Why do I keep saying Rougarou?" Suddenly, the woman's stomach began to turn as she doubled over in pain. Pulling the IV from her arm, she allowed herself to fall from the bed while her ankles dangled in purgatory between the mattress and the floor. Glancing up at the clock on the wall, she looked at the time. "It's almost 8:30. I've got to get out of here." Rolling over onto her stomach, Kasey began to pull and claw towards the door. Small beads of sweat formed on her forehead as the bed rocked back and forth, teetering between regaining its position and toppling over altogether. "Shit, shit, shit..." She chanted as she pounded on the floor with her fists. She felt weak and tired already. Unless

31

someone came to her aid, she didn't know what her next step would be.

There, she laid on the floor. At some point, she rolled back over on her back and stared at the ceiling, counting the bumps and ridges on the popcorn finish. Fiddling with the hem of her medical gown, she glanced at the clock one more time. It was only a matter of minutes before that horrible man would be back donning a rather nasty cocktail of poison to put in her arm. The beeps on the machines began to quicken as she heard a set of footsteps approaching the door. Was this it? Was this how she was going to die?

Rolling over onto her side, she watched whoever was on the other side fiddle with the lock. The overhead lights buzzed, and for some reason, it was all Kasey could hear as that tickle in her brain came back with a vengeance. Seconds later, the door creaked open, and for the first time she could remember, Kasey could take a good look out into the hallway. It didn't look anything like she thought it would. It was dank and dreary. A little red light hung loosely from the ceiling fixture between two PVC pipes. She could hear the dripping of what she hoped was water somewhere in the distance. It was like two worlds: her white hospital room and the one that lay beyond. It was surreal and almost unbelievable.

"Hello?" Kasey called as she squinted towards the door. "Who's there?" There was movement just out of her line of sight. Something large and heavy hit something much softer, and moments later, the man in the white coat fell to the ground. He had a rather nasty bump on the head, but Kasey could tell he was still alive. His chest moved up and down in a slow but rhythmic motion. She could feel the hairs on the back of her neck stand on end as a metal pipe fell to the ground with a bang somewhere in the darkness. "Who's there?" Kasey called as she pulled on the chains harder.

"No need for the dramatics!" A woman replied just out of her line of sight. "I was a bit tied up... Literally. It took a second to get to you. Are you alright?"

"I'm stuck!" Kasey called back. Finally, a woman entered the room. She was smaller and younger than Kasey would have imagined. She was a slight girl with magnificent cinnamon-colored locks. Her eyes matched, and they shimmered even in the weird light. Kneeling beside the unconscious man, she fished around in his pockets, finally pulling out a keychain.

Rushing to Kasey's side, she opened her restraints and helped Kasey to her feet.

"Goodness, Ms. Tomlin, you were a hard one to find. I wish you would have met with me before all of this had gotten so out of control."

"I'm sorry, I don't remember. I don't know what happened or who you think I am." Grabbing Kasey's hand, the woman smiled and pulled her towards the door.

"My name is Smita Chatter, and I've been trying to reach you about your car's extended warranty." Grimacing, the woman rolled her eyes and looked down at the man in the doorway.

"No, seriously, what's going on?" Eyeballing the blood bag on the floor, Smita groaned and shook her head.

"They've been poisoning you. Trying to get you to forget."

"Forget what?" Kasey asked. Smita dragged the woman from the room and down the hall. Every so often, she would pass an unconscious person in a white coat; all of them had the same logo embroidered on the right breast pocket. Smita had been a busy girl, and Kasey wasn't ungrateful for the save, but she still didn't quite understand why she was worth saving... Or how she knew what a Rougarou was.

"I'll try to fill you in on the basics. I'm sure you'll get most of your senses back after this allergy wears off. You're name is Kasey Tomlin, and you own a floral shop on Orchard."

"I know that much. What I don't get is how I got here."

"One word... Espionage. I've only been in the states for about five months, but your name has come up in more than one or two conversations. You're pretty famous here in the procurement of black-market hexes, remedies and wards. I didn't know I was being followed."

"I don't think I follow," Kasey said as she touched the corner of her head and closed her eyes. She was doing everything in her power to keep from falling over. Bouts of nausea were rushing over her like waves on the beach.

"I think it's around the corner here... Yes!" Smita said with a giggle. "We're almost out of here." Looking over her shoulder, the woman frowned as she watched Kasey wobble a little on her toes before leaning against the wall.

"We might need to take a quick break." She began.

"No! We don't have that kind of time. It's not much further. I parked around the corner before I let them capture me."

35

"You LET them?" Kasey asked with amazement. "Weren't you scared?" Laughing, Smita waved a hand at the woman and pulled her back to her feet.

"Not really. Humans are much more predictable than cryptids. I figured they'd let their guard down eventually. After moving here, I needed to put down roots. I found this girl, Beatrice, she's great. I live with her now, about five blocks from your shop. Maybe you two should meet up sometime... Or maybe not." Pushing the rusted door open with her free hand, Smita dragged Kasey out into the warm fall night. "We don't have a lot of time; I'm sure they'll be on us as soon as one of those goons wakes up." Kasey could hear the door behind them click shut. Her mind felt foggy, but she allowed the woman to pull her down the street and around the corner. What else was she supposed to do? Obviously, a lot had happened, and she couldn't remember any of it.

Like Smita had promised, a white van was parked down a dark alley around the corner from the unmarked building they had left. Loading into it, the two girls drove off into the night, away from town and any signs of life. Leaning back into her seat, Kasey put a hand on her head and groaned as her stomach began to turn.

"I think I'm going to be sick." She moaned.

"I would appreciate it if you didn't. I just had her cleaned." Smita began.

"You've got to help me remember what happened. I don't remember anything. It's driving me crazy." Thinking momentarily, the woman took a right beside the old library and nodded silently.

"So, all you remember is that you own that flower shop? You can't recollect anything else?" Shrugging her shoulders, Kasey moaned again and closed her eyes as the van hit a rather large pothole.

"Could you not do that... Unless you changed your mind and want me to paint your floorboard." Opening her eyes a little, she glanced at the driver and smirked. "I do remember this big dog-looking thing."

"It was a Rougarou."

"A Rougarou?"

"Yeah, that's the thing that bit you. I think it wanted you dead."

"Why would it want to do that? Not to mention, I put Devil's Shoestring over the doorway... Wait, how do I know that'll keep them out?"

"Your memory must be coming back. That's a good thing. I know a lot, but you'll have to fill in some of the missing pieces." Tightening the grip on her steering wheel, Smita wrinkled her nose and slowed down at the red light.

"Wait, that man in the white coat, I think I know his name. Was it Davis... Something."

"Yeah, that was Davis Kellerman. He's the head honcho at Lupin Corp., Human trafficking for cryptids and oddballs. Lupin Corp wants to use your gifts and those of others like you to enhance their DNA. I guess, since the discovery of the boogeyman, Davis has been looking for his own God Particle." Turning towards the Moondust Tunnel, Smita slowed down the van and looked at the woman in the passenger seat.

"You're not serious, are you? The Boogeyman doesn't exist... Does it." Smirking, Smita tapped her finger on the dash and shrugged at Kasey.

"Wouldn't you like to know?"

"Well... Yeah... That's why I asked."

"Coming from you, that's a hilarious statement. Seeing as most of the people around here might call you that."

"I'm... I'm sorry. I still don't follow." Closing her eyes, Kasey leaned back into the seat, grabbing her belly with both hands. "If I don't get to a bathroom soon, I'm afraid I won't be able to keep whatever's inside from coming out, clean upholstery or not." Smita could hear her new friend's stomach begin to growl again as she moaned quietly to herself.

"You came here about a year ago. I followed not long after. I wanted to keep a close eye on someone like you. You're special, you know... Or maybe you don't. Kasey Tomlin died about twenty years ago, not to diminish the fact that you're still very much Kasey, just new and improved. Before you died, you were a pretty amazing green witch, and you did pretty much the same job you do now. When people needed protection from all things dark and wicked, you were there with a bag or a potion." Leaning in, Smita elbowed the woman in the passenger seat. "I haven't seen it myself, but I have a few buddies that swore you knew how to fight back with nothing more than a hanging fern. In any case, you were poisoned, and eventually, you succumbed to it."

"Well, if I died, then how come I can walk and talk... Am I a zombie??!?" Burping loudly, Kasey opened her eyes wide and covered her mouth as her cheeks began to turn red. "Excuse me."

"It's okay," Smita said as they exited the tunnel, "that's to be expected. I can't believe they filled you full of blood... What with your condition."

"You keep saying stuff like that. What do you mean?" grabbing the door handle, Kasey rolled the window down as fast as she could. Hanging her head out, she began to vomit. Smita patiently waited for her to stop before she continued.

"I'll tell you all I know on the subject. Please don't take everything I say as gospel truth because I wasn't there for the transformation. You see, when you died, the people of Hollow Grove didn't take the news very well. You were something of a local legend and you made quite a bit of an impression on one very striking and charismatic necromancer named Peter. Needless to say, he was the only one equipped to handle your... condition. His idea was pulling your soul back into your body, but the flesh had already started to rot away. He knew, in time, your cognitive functions would diminish, and you wouldn't be you anymore... Not really. That's where Sasha came in. Against the council's better judgment, she also came to your aid. Sasha was an elder vampire, and while uncommon, her type held the secret to eternal youth, and she gifted a little of hers to you." Pulling down the visor, Kasey looked into it, gasping in surprise.

"My eyes! Why are they black? They used to be blue."

"Yeah, about that. When the Rougarou bit you, your eyes kind of did that. It might be a part of your condition, or it might be something completely unrelated."

"My condition... MY condition? What exactly IS MY CONDITION? You're dancing around it. Spit it out already." Sighing, Smita pulled into her apartment's parking garage and started rounding the corners.

"That's just the thing. We've never seen it before. I've been watching you at Lupin Corp for days, and there's no way to fix it... At least no way we've discovered. When you got bit the night you came home from work, and the Wolf was waiting, his tooth broke off into your neck. Someone had to have starved it and then lured it there. When you were brought back the first time, Peter and Sasha speculated that Davis and his goons had tried to kill you for protecting the monsters they were trying to kidnap. Your friends pooled their money and moved you across the country in hopes that Lupin Corp wouldn't pick up on your scent, which worked for a while. I think Davis was unaware of your cryptid status. He may have thought you had simply faked your own death and gone underground to continue the resistance. I think the Rougarou was planted in your house to kill you by Davis and the Corporation once again. Like most devious indignations, this one was half-cooked, and I had gotten the heads up before too long. Unfortunately, I wasn't there fast enough to stop the attack, and the monster's cross-contamination, leaving a bit of itself inside you, gave you the same debilitating disease the monster's human form probably has as well."

"And what's that exactly?"

"Here in the living world, we simply call it Alpha-Gal. It comes from a tick bite." Pulling into a parking space, Smita turned off the engine and looked over at Kasey with concern.

"So, what you're saying is a flea-ridden dog with bad teeth attacked me, and now I'm a…"

"A Vegan Vampire."

Chapter four
The ABCs of Cryptid Combat

"Who is 'she,' and why is she asleep so late at night?" Tom asked as he watched his tiny captors exit the van. Walking around, Smita rushed around the van and grabbed my arm before I had a chance to confront Tom.

"Ouch! What are you doing?" I asked as I wrinkled my nose.

"I told you about bringing strays home. It never ends well."

"He followed me out into the parking lot! I didn't know the Squonk had escaped. It wasn't like I fed him or anything. Smita... you don't think I asked him to come along, do you?" Letting go of my arm, Smita frowned and shuffled her feet.

"I don't know what I'm thinking right now. All I know for sure is we're stuck with him for a little while longer... BUT! He's your puppy. You clean up his messes."

"Hey!" Tom exclaimed as he climbed out of the back of the van. "I can hear you; you know... And I'm potty trained..." Looking over her shoulder, Smita smiled and nodded, grabbing the man's hand.

"Sure, you are, buddy, and we're just so proud of you." Pulling him along, I watched Smita stop towards the elevator. I lingered in the back, keeping to myself the best I could. Smita wasn't wrong. Bringing people back from hunts usually ended in disaster, and it was rule one of Cryptid Combat. People don't usually take to the news that they aren't the only intelligent life walking around very well. Me included.

"Are we going up to your apartment?" Tom asked as Smita smashed the button to the elevator with her finger.

"Not yet. I need to talk to Kasey. We couldn't get the Squonk, and you know what that means."

"Oh, God, is it gonna come back for us?" Tom asked as he shuddered, thinking back to the parking lot.

"Not exactly. We watched Lupin Corp eyeballing it for a while now and they only snatch the beasts they intend on using."

"Lupin Corp? Do you mean the financial firm down on Grand? What do they have to do with anything." Laughing, Smita pulled the boy through the open elevator door as I followed quickly behind. Pressing the up button, Smita let go of Tom and crossed her arms, deep in thought.

"Change of plans; I'll go see Kasey, and you two head for the apartment. Tell Tom everything he needs to know... But ONLY the things he needs to know. He probably wants to go home sometime soon without constantly looking over his shoulder." Nodding my head, I kept quiet and watched as the others bantered back and forth. The elevator bounced and wobbled with each floor it passed. Finally, the door dinged open, and Smita pushed us out into the hallway. "I won't be long. Stay in the apartment, and don't open the door for anyone." Leaning forward, Tom placed his hands on his hips and stomped his feet. The doors to the elevator began to close again, but that didn't stop him from getting in the last word.

"Don't tell us what to do, Smita! You're not our real mom!" I couldn't help but grin a little as the look on Smita's face changed from snarky to surprised.

"I don't think I've heard anyone talk to her like that before." Laughing nervously, Tom ran a hand through his dark hair and rolled his eyes.

He had lost his hair tie somewhere between the parking lot and the apartment. The locks that framed his face highlighted his hazel eyes. The more I looked at him, the more I realized he wasn't a bad-looking guy. Waving my hand, I started walking to the apartment, shoving my hand in my pocket; I hoped I hadn't left my keys on the counter again.

"Your friend is super intense. Why do you hang out with her?"

"She's not that bad," I replied, stopping in front of door 111. "We just have a lot going on." Touching the handle, I stopped for a moment. Holding the key in the other hand, I stared at the door with concern.

"Is something wrong?" Tom asked as he approached me from behind.

"I don't know," I replied. Shoving the key into the lock, I tried my best to shake off the feeling, but no matter how hard I tried, the hairs on the back of my neck wouldn't lay down. The door to the apartment creaked open, and the only thing on the other side there to greet us was darkness and the faint aroma of lavender.

"Cozy," Tom said as he brushed past me, crossing the threshold and flicking on the light. "You got anything to eat? It's past my dinner time." Taking a deep breath, I jammed the keys back into my pocket and walked through the door, shutting and locking it behind me.

"Please," I began with an eye-roll, "make yourself at home." Flopping down on the couch, Tom crossed his legs and closed his eyes. For a second, I thought he was going to drift off to sleep, but moments later, he was alert and full of questions.

"What's a Squonk, and why does it smell so bad? Why were you two hunting it? Why haven't I seen you before if you live so close? Do you have any pizza?" Laughing, I lifted my hands in surrender and met up with him on the couch. I knew I owed the man a bit of an explanation but didn't know how he would take it.

"My name is Beatrice Bones, and I'm a student at Moondust College. My friend in the basement is Smita Chatter. We met a while ago when I was looking for a roommate. Turns out this company, Lupin Corp, is in the business of genetic mutation. They have no regard or respect for the life of anyone other than themselves. Smita moved here from overseas to continue her father's work. A long time ago, a cryptid took Smita in and raised her as their own after her father died in a war he didn't start. This power struggle has been going on for a long

47

time, and I want to be on the right side of history. It doesn't hurt that I'm writing my dissertation, Kasey." Thinking back to the day we met, I couldn't have imagined myself being so close to a creature of the night.

"Who's Kasey?" Tom asked as he scooted closer to the edge of the couch. Crossing his arms, the man waited for my response.

"Alright, buckle up because it's a bumpy ride. Kasey Tomlin is a Vegan Vampire. She started out in this world as a powerful green witch. Lupin Corp hates her because she's been weaponizing the very creatures they've come to collect. They killed her once, but a powerful necromancer and an original vampire brought her back. They tried again to killer again many years later, but it didn't work. In the process, though, she contracted a blood disorder that makes her extremely allergic to mammal meat or blood." Lowering his brow, Tom tilted his head with concern.

"But… Then how does she eat? Is she all gross and wrinkly? Will she turn to dust soon?"

"No," I replied with a smirk. "We load her down with Vitamin D tablets. Vampirism is simply an inability to absorb vitamin D from the sun, you know, cause… POOF! Her bloodlust subsides once she's had enough, and she's good to go. Of course, her super strength and night vision suffer a bit because of it, but until I can synthesis something better, that has to do." Suddenly, the lights flickered and cut off completely. The hair on the back of my neck stood up again, and I immediately grabbed Tom's hand.

"Wow... It's probably just a rolling backout. It happens sometimes."

"In this line of work, nothing is just... Nothing." Fumbling to get to my feet, I pulled Tom along, hoping to make it to my room, but all my hopes were dashed when I heard the window in the kitchen smash, and an eerie sound filled my ears. It was a familiar sound, one I had heard not long ago. "Is that a baby crying?" I whispered. Looking over my shoulder, I watched Tom's face. Even in the darkness, I could see the horror in his eyes.

"Why would someone throw their baby into a fourth-story window?" He whispered back. I could tell that the man still hadn't grasped the seriousness of it all. The air in the room began to rush around us, and the temperature dropped ten degrees. I could feel goosebumps as they rose along the tops of my arms.

"I can't believe they got one."

"Got what?"

"A Wendigo." Running for the bedroom, I pulled Tom through with all my might. Knocking him onto the bed I turned my back to him and began pulling on my old computer desk. "We've got to keep it out long enough for Smita and Kasey to discover what's going on."

"Don't you have a phone or something you can call them?" Tom asked as he regained his balance. Rushing to my side, he grabbed the back of the desk and helped me pull. It began to slide a few inches towards us but then stopped in its tracks. The computer cords were holding it steadfast to its home.

"The basement is lined in lead. Probably used to be a bunker during the cold war or something. There's no cell phone reception down there. I don't have one anyway because this one time while me and Smita were hunting, I got to meet a Raiju. It zapped me pretty good."

"A... What?" Tom asked, but before I could answer, the bedroom door flew from its hinges and across the living room floor. It found a home against the front door, pressed heavily against the handle. "We're screwed, aren't we?" Tom asked bluntly. Nodding, I closed my eyes as the crying grew louder and louder. With every passing minute, the room grew colder. Goosebumps began to form on my neck and the back of my arms. Scrambling to his feet, Tom ran to my side and attempted to look over my shoulder into the darkness. "I don't see anything." Tom began, but seconds later, he was silenced as something big and awkward lumbered through the kitchen.

"Do you see it now?" I asked silently. The man nodded as he put a hand on my shoulder.

The monster was just like the book had described. The Wendigo paced the floor by the open window, dodging the warm night air. It stood a good seven feet tall, hunching over so as not to hit it's giant, animal skull of a cranium on our popcorn ceiling. The smell was indescribable, almost like warm saltwater and rotten meat. Even though the foul demon had no eyes, I could tell that it could see through some sort of dark magic, and it sniffed the air, attempting to find its next victim. Reaching out a ragged hand, the thing touched the hanging plants by the window it had destroyed, watching with morbid pleasure as the little ferns swayed against its touch. On the end of each finger, nestled a very shiny, dark red nail that was in desperate need of a manicure.

"What do we do?" Tom whispered with panic in his voice. I didn't have to turn around to know that the man's giant hazel eyes were set, unblinking on the Wendigo. If it had been a year earlier, I would have reacted the same way. Craning my neck, I looked over my shoulder and locked eyes with my house mate.

"I'm not sure. I haven't quite reached the W's in my required reading. Of course, I've skimmed the book a few times and admired the graphics... We've got to wait for Smita and Kasey... I'm sure they'll know what to do." Suddenly Tom tightened his grip on my shoulder as his eyes widened. Even in our situation, it was hard for me not to find the humor in his expression. It didn't take long for my own smug grin to vanish when Tom said four small words.

"Where did it go?" Turning around slowly, I let out a deep breath. The air was so cold now I could see the steam rising from my nostrils. It felt as though time had stopped, and you could hear a pin drop. The silence was deafening. Squinting my eyes, I looked for the beast, but Tom was right. It had vanished into thin air. "Do you think it jumped back out of the window?" He asked, but I shook my head. I couldn't share the same hope as my partner because the temps in the room had continued to drop, and I was about five seconds away from pulling my winter coat out of the closet.

There was a rustling from behind me, and then I heard Tom make an exaggerated sound. It was almost as if he were going to scream, and something shoved a sock into his mouth. Swinging around to face him, I watched in crippling horror as the skull-faced freak that had broken into my apartment swung Tom around like a rag doll. I didn't know how it had gotten past us, but it didn't really matter at this point.

"Let him go!" I yelped as I snatched the table lamp from my desk. Lifting it over my head, I heard everything else on the table beginning to fall to the floor. Wrinkling my nose, I remembered the surge protector everything on my desk was plugged into and could only guess how many pieces of gear were now on the floor, possibly ruined. Pulling on the cord, I managed to wriggle the lamp free before I lobbed it at the Wendigo's head. It bounced off the corner of its nose with a plink as it fell to the ground by my feet. "Take that, you cannibalistic freak!" I wasn't sure if it was my valiant yet stupid attempt at stopping the monster that got its attention or if it had just had enough of toying with Tom, but in any case, it threw the man across the room and came lumbering towards me. Tom's head hit the grate as he moaned. His eyes rolled up into the back of his head, and his body went limp just as the Wendigo snatched me up by my arm. Kicking the desk out of the way, the monster dragged me across the floor, snorting, and then opened its mouth, letting out another cry. This time, it sounded much more terrifying.

"Tom! Tom, I need you to listen very carefully. Do I have your attention?" Moaning, Tom lifted his head as strands of dark hair matted themselves against his forehead. Reaching up, he touched the corner of his temple and winced. There was a deep gash, and it had begun to bleed pretty badly.

"Who's in the grate?" Tom mumbled. He could barely keep his eyes open. Even though he wanted to more than anything, his eyes just wouldn't adjust.

"I know we haven't officially met yet, but it's me, Kasey. Smita and I have been sidetracked. We'll get to you as soon as possible, but until then, could you do me a solid? Can you do that for me?" Tom inched closer to the grate, lowering his brows and smashing his face against the opening.

"You gotta be awfully tiny to be in there."

"I'm not in the wall, Tom. I'm still in the basement, I just know which heating unit is Smita's. Listen, your scent is getting stronger, which can only mean one thing... You're bleeding, aren't you?"

"Maaayybbeee," Tom said with a snicker.

"Oh my God... Smita, can you talk to this goon for me?" There was a bit of a shuffle as the two women whispered back and forth for a moment. Wedging his fingers through the opening in the metal cover, Tom pulled on the grate to no avail.

"Listen, Tom, you need to get as close to the Wendigo as you can and whistle. They hate that. Is that something you can do for me?"

"I'm naming him Steve. I think he looks like a Steve."

"TOMMY! I NEED YOU TO GO SAVE MY FRIEND IN THERE! CAN YOU DO THAT?" Blinking hard, Tom finally managed to stumble to his feet and walk towards the bedroom door. Squinting his eyes, he could see the blurry figure swinging me around. I was swaying and flailing about like one of those god-awful pharmacy receipts in the wind. Every time I would open my mouth to scream, I would be shit-whipped in a different direction, and all the air would be knocked out of my sails. Finally, when I thought I couldn't take it any longer, the monster stopped. Holding me out in front of it like a trophy. Tilting it's head to the side, it gave some sort of animated smile, boring a hole through me with its ice-cold stare. I didn't know what it was doing, but something new was in the air. It filled my nose with a sensation I had never had before. It tingled all the senses I had, and then the realization hit me... I hadn't eaten all day.

Chapter five
Basement Confessionals

The elevator to the bottom floor opened, and Smita hopped off. Making her way down the hall, she passed door after door. Each one was closed with a little black marker across the middle that stated in bold, ' OFFICE USE ONLY' or 'AUTHORIZED PERSONELLE ONLY.' Smita knew what was on the other side of each one. Most of them were either empty or held cleaning supplies for the apartment staff to use. In the very back, there was a room with an open door and on the inside of that door was Kasey's lair. Smita always giggled when she used the term, but there wasn't another word for it. She could make out the grow lights in the far back, where Kasey continued with her horticulture. It was part of their agreement.

After Smita had saved the vegan vampire from a fate worse than death, Kasey eventually got most of her memories back. She remembered Davis Hellerman and his nefarious attempt at murder. It hadn't taken long for the night-stalking temptress to want to break free from Smita's tight embrace. She had things to do and Cryptids to save. Smita had other plans, though.

"Come and stay here with us. We can work together. Three heads are better than one."

"I don't want to put you into harm's way any more than I already have," Kasey replied as she crossed her arms. Handing the woman a little bottle of pills, Smita put her hands on her hips and tapped her foot.

"You've been here a month already, and nothing has happened. As long as you stay in the basement, Birdie and I can get the cryptids out of town, and you can arm the ones that can defend themselves. I can get them to you." Pointing a finger to the ceiling, Smita smiled and winked. "The lady that lives above you is like a hundred years old and deaf. You can make as much noise as you want; she would never notice. Other than that, we are here alone. I can get you whatever you need, and you can continue your work here." Kasey thought it over and ultimately agreed. Kasey said it was because her cover had been blown at the flower shop, but Smita knew better. Kasey needed friends. She had been alone for so long that she craved the connection.

Walking to the end of the hall, Smita popped her head through the open door and looked around. Everything was quiet except for the low hum of the electrical wiring that hung loosely over her head. All of Kasey's plants were in full bloom, even the ones that were out of season. It was good to know that the transformation had done little to stifle her green witch prowess.

"Hey, Kasey, you in here?" Smita called as she walked through the threshold. "I have some bad news; we didn't get the Squonk. I figured it's in the wind, though, so she should be safe for the time being. We met up with this guy at the local store, and he jacked things up for us. Now he's tagging along like Birdie's cheerleader. Honestly, he's cramping my style. Any way you could scare him into running away? Kasey?" Walking further into the room, Smita pursed her lips and listened with all her might. Far off into the back of the lead-lined lair, she could hear two people whispering. She couldn't make out what they were saying, but she could tell that they were not in agreeance.

"You can't seriously ask me to do that. It's a death sentence."

"I wouldn't have asked you if I had any other choice... Plus, your basically unkillable, right?" The closer the woman got, the clearer the conversation was becoming. The first voice she recognized was Kasey's, but the second one was new, female, and filled with fear.

"You know what I do here. My work doesn't go any deeper than the cryptids and creatures that can't defend themselves."

"Yeah, well, that all changed when you did what you did last week. I can't believe you went there, Kasey. I thought you had more sense than that."

"Well, someone had to do something! Davis was there, and Sally. They were like sitting ducks. Haven't you heard of cutting off the head of the snake? I thought what I was doing was for the greater good."

"Who's there!" Smita called as she walked towards the back corner of the basement. Kasey had hung up a white sheet to block out the light from the grow lamps in the corner where her bed had been placed. Unfortunately, the light did nothing, and the silhouettes behind the stunted sheet were invisible. Reaching out, Smita grabbed the cloth and pulled it back, exposing the two behind it. Kasey looked surprised, her black eyes glistening in the faint light of the lamps behind Smita, but the other woman was less than impressed with the girl's interruption.

Pointing a finger at Smita, she frowned and waggled it a few times.

"Who the hell is this? Your bodyguard? Or was SHE the one who thought crashing a board meeting in the center of Lupin Corp was a good idea?"

"You did WHAT now?" Smita asked as her mouth hung open in shock. "I thought I told you to lay low. I thought we were using the back door to take down this company, Kasey; now they KNOW for a FACT you're still out here doing.... All of this. What if they followed you? What if they know about me.... Worse yet, what if they know about Birdie? I left her upstairs unprotected, unprepared." Turning around, Smita ran for the open doorway, but the new girl was much faster. She was in front of Smita in a matter of seconds, slamming the door shut behind her. Pressing her body against the lead enclosure, she shook her head.

"You're not going anywhere. We've got too much to discuss." Pushing past Smita, Kasey walked between the two of them and hissed with aggression.

"I've never threatened violence on you, Neith, but so help me, if you touch a hair on this woman's head, I'll have to do just that."

"Neith?" Smita said as she lowered her brow. "I think I've heard of you…. I just can't quite put my finger on it." Smiling, the young woman took a few steps closer and held out her hand. "I'm Neith Lupin. Sorry for the late introduction." Looking into the woman's yellow eyes, Smita backed away closer to Kasey. There was something about her that was both alluring and frightening at the same time.

Neith Lupin was a slight girl with pale skin and long dark hair she kept back in a loose braid. She couldn't have been more than nineteen, with high cheekbones and eyes that could see into your soul. Neith had full, pouty lips that barely opened when she talked, but every word she said dripped with sexuality and heat. If the air hit her just right, Smita could smell the sea upon her skin, salty and fresh, and she walked in waves like the rolling tide of the water she emerged from. Neith wasn't like the other cryptids she had worked with before. She had an air about her that exuded confidence and royalty. Every movement Neith made was with intent and purpose. In the end, Smita knew for a fact that the woman in front of her was no cryptid at all but something much darker and more threatening.

"You have to excuse Neith; she's a byproduct of the runoff in Hollowtail River. Just one of the mutations that escaped the dumping ground. Neith likes to think of herself as the daughter of an Old God... One who's sleeping not fifty miles south of here." Smiling slyly, Neith pressed her body against the closed door and sighed with the dreaminess of a cat on a warm windowsill.

"I don't think it, I KNOW it, Kasey. Don't be jealous that there's more than one special person in the room. If it weren't for you, I wouldn't be here at all asking for a favor. You're the one who started this, and you should be the one to finish it." Turning her head towards Kasey, Smita frowned and crossed her arms.

"What did you start? Why is this woman here, and what does she want you to do?" Backing away slowly, Kasey put her hands out in front of her as one of the grow lights in the corner popped.

"Okay, I'll tell you, but you can't get your panties in a wad."

"Panties in a wad? When do I ever do that?" Smita stated as she tapped her foot on the hard ground below her.

"I rarely wear panties... Such a restraining piece of clothing."

"Neith!" Kasey snapped as she pointed a finger in her friend's direction. "Now isn't the time." Nodding, the woman pushed a small piece of hair behind her ear and allowed Kasey to continue. "Look... Smita, I wouldn't have gone if I hadn't have thought I could handle it."

"But clearly, you didn't. Isn't that why this... girl is here now?" Grimacing, Smita looked over her shoulder at the sultry vixen and hoped against all hope that Tom never laid eyes on her.

"Well, yes and no. It's true that I went to Lupin Corp on my own last night. You two were busy looking for the Squonk and I didn't want you to take your minds off of what was really important." Wagging a finger in Kasey's direction, Smita shook her head and frowned.

"No, you didn't tell us because you know what we would say. It's stupid! You've put us all in danger."

"That wasn't my intention! I got it on good authority that Sally Watkins was coming in from the island. She's been illuding us until now. I knew that something was up, Smita. I could smell it in the air. I waited until the cover of night, and I walked right into that stupid little financial firm. I intended to stay out of sight, but I couldn't... Not after." Suddenly, a sound echoed through the grates of the basement.

Turning her attention to the small opening in the wall, Smita ran to it, pressing her ear against the wire mesh.

"Something is up there with them, Kasey! They're up there alone. We need to go." Something far off in the distance began to howl as cold air rushed against Smita's face. Jumping back, the woman gasped in surprise. "A Wendigo? How the hell did a Wendigo get upstairs?"

"Probably through a window. I doubt it had a key." Shooting daggers in Neith's direction, Smita watched the woman transform in front of her eyes. The once smoldering beauty had become something of an eyesore. Her braid had turned into tentacles, and the pupils in her eyes elongated like that of an octopus. Her once milky white skin quickly became grey and slimy, almost see-through. The dark veins that webbed out just underneath were an odd and unnerving shade of blue. Even through the transformation, Smita's face never changed. She was unphased by it, only wanting to get to her friends and stop the monster from unleashing an age-old curse upon them.

Running towards the two at the door, Smita held out her hands, ready to push Neith out of the way, but Kasey stopped her.

"I know you want to get to Birdie, but this isn't the way. Neith can take your face off with one bite."

"Let us out of here, and we'll do whatever you want us to do! I can't lose my friend." Smirking, Neith began to shrink down as she wedged herself under the door.

"I believe that coming from you, but I need to hear it from Kasey. She's the only one that can get him out, and I need him to be free. It's just not right." Seconds later, the woman was on the other side of the door, and only a second after that, the door clicked, signaling a lock. Grabbing her friend by the collar, Smita shook Kasey with all her strength.

"Tell her you'll do it! Whatever she wants you to do, just tell her you will."

"I take my word pretty seriously, Smita, and I can't do that. You don't understand what she's asking... You don't know the whole story." Suddenly, something from above hit the wall hard, as a low moan emanated through the pipes. "I've got a better idea, but you're just going to have to trust me." Letting go of Kasey, Smita nodded sullenly. "Good, now go to my herbal garden over there and look for a jar labeled Nanajuju. I need it. While you're there,

I'll try to talk some sense into that man up there."

"His name is Tom. He's kind of a durp." Running to the table, Smita looked around at the jars and elixirs Kasey had labeled. She had left them scattered about, and there were a lot of them. Running to the wire mesh, Kasey pulled it off, throwing it onto the floor at her feet. Getting up on her tippy toes, she pressed her face against the opening and began to yell.

"Tom, Tom, I need you to listen very carefully. Do I have your attention?"

"Who's in the grate?" The man moaned as he shifted his weight closer to the opening.

"I know we haven't officially met yet, but it's me, Kasey. Smita and I have been sidetracked. We'll get to you as soon as we can, but until then, could you do me a solid? Can you do that for me?"

"I don't see it!" Smita screamed as she fished through the sea of never-ending glass jars. "What color is this, Nanajuju?"

"You've gotta be awfully tiny to be in there." Rolling her eyes, Kasey pressed her face further into the opening.

"I'm not in the wall, Tom. I'm still in the basement. I just know which heating unit is Smita's. Listen, your scent is getting, which can

67

only mean one thing... Your bleeding, aren't you?"

"Maaayybbeee," Tom replied and then snorted heavily.

"I found it!" Smita said as she held up a bottle of milky white nastiness. "What do you want me to do now?" Holding out her hand, Kasey motioned for Smita to come closer.

"Oh my God... Smita, can you talk to this goon for me?" Handing the vial to Kasey, the woman gave her a half-amused glance.

"I told you he was a bit of a durp. He's the whole reason we lost the Squonk and..."

"We don't have time for this!" Kasey exclaimed as she popped the top and downed the concoction. Wrinkling her nose, Smita took Kasey's place at the opening, pressing her face into the dust-covered ductwork.

"Listen, Tom, you need to get as close to the Wendigo as you can and whistle. They hate that. Is that something you can do for me?"

"I'm naming him Steve. I think he looks like a Steve."

"TOMMY! I NEED YOU TO GO SAVE MY FRIEND IN THERE! CAN YOU DO THAT?" Smita waited for a response but nothing came. All she could do now was hope that Tom would do as she said until they could figure out how to get out of their lead-lined coffins. Turning to face Kasey, she watched the woman fish through the plants she had been growing. Finally, she smiled, pulling a few stems from a red and green plant.

"What's that?" Smita asked.

"It's mandragora. Thought I might take a little with me. You remember where my drums are, right?" Nodding, Smita walked around the white sheet. Seconds later, she came out with two small hand drums attached to a strap.

"This is all well and good, but where are you going exactly? Did that stuff you drink give you super strength? Are we busting out of here?" Shaking her head, Kasey pointed to the grate.

"I'm going through there. Once the Nanajuju has time to synthesize in my system, I'll turn to smoke."

"You'll WHAT?" Smita asked in amazement. "For how long? Do you have any more of that stuff?"

"I don't know how long I'll be like that... And don't even think about drinking it yourself, Smita. I need you down here playing the drums. That potion is for immortals only. It would kill you dead." Pursing her lips, Smita nodded silently as she watched Kasey slowly dissolve into thin air. The smoke was grey and blue, and

69

it reminded Smita of vape discharge. Moving out of the way, she watched Kasey vanish through the opening.

"Here goes nothing," Smita said to herself. Throwing the strap over her shoulder, Smita positioned the hand drums carefully onto her side and began to play. The thick Hyde instrument echoed louder and louder against the thick walls around her. It wouldn't be long now, she thought, before they were all in a trance, and Kasey could really do some damage.

Chapter six
The Wendigo has got to go.

The Wendigo pointed to the man in the doorway, setting me down on the floor beside it. For some reason, I didn't see Tom anymore. He looked more like a bloody rare steak, and I hadn't eaten in a month. I could feel the drool as it began to fall from the corners of my mouth. There was nothing I could do about it. It was almost as if I were under a powerful spell.

Taking a few steps closer, I watched with entertainment as Tom struggled to keep his footing. Reaching up, the man put two fingers into his mouth and blew, but nothing came out.

"I've never been good at stuff like this." He muttered, using his good hand to hold onto the doorway. Taking his fingers out of his mouth, he inspected them, shook them around a few times, and stuck them back into the corner of his mouth.

"What are you waiting for?" A voice asked. It wasn't a voice I had heard before and didn't sound like it was in the room. Shaking my head back and forth, I stuck a finger in my ear and wriggled it around.

"Get out of there!" I exclaimed, but the voice just laughed at my response.

"You invited me in! Is this how you treat all your house guests?" Forcing my attention away from Tom, I looked up at the Wendigo. It hadn't moved from the spot it had been standing in. It hadn't taken any interest in the bleeding man in the doorway or attempted to pick me back up. The Wendigo hadn't done anything in the last thirty seconds other than stare down at me with empty eyes, but something in my heart knew that the little voice inside my head was the monster, and it was communicating with me for a reason.

"I didn't invite you in! You broke through the window and knocked all my furniture around. You threw Tom across the room and hurt him! I want you gone now!" Pointing a finger at the skull-faced freak, I nodded toward the window and tapped my foot. "So, go on now. What are you waiting for?"

Cocking its head to one side, I thought I could see the Wendigo smirk. It was a weird sensation, seeing a reaction on the face of death... But there it was, standing in the middle of my ruined living room.

"I can't leave now. We're just starting to have a little fun."

"What does that even mean?" I asked, but I didn't have to wait for an answer. I could feel the hairs on the back of my neck rising as I sniffed the air. Tom was making his way closer to us and it was all I could to hold my ground. The Wendigo's curse made me hunger for human flesh, and the cut on the man's head only made things worse.

"Go on now. Get us a little dinner."

"Hey, Birdie, who are you talking to over there? Can you whistle?" Tom stumbled towards us, stopping just on the other side of the couch. His dark hair was matted heavily against his temple, but the gash was still very noticeable. It stopped just above his left eyebrow, and it was weeping.

"You need to stay as far away from me as possible, Tom! I don't know how long I can hold on."

"What are you talking about?" Tom motioned for me to come to him. Even though he was clearly unsteady on his feet, he was doing the best he could to help. "Steve isn't good for you. I think you two should call it quits." The smell of warm blood in the air made my body shake with excitement. I ran my tongue against my teeth, trying to reel in the saliva. They had grown sharp and deadly. I wanted nothing more in this world than to take a big bite out of Tom's soft, succulent flesh.

"He's right there." The Wendigo began. "All you have to do is walk over and take it. Then you can be like me forever." Balling my hands into fists, I tried to skirt the urge. I think it would have worked too... If Tom hadn't leaned over the couch. I had turned on my heels before I knew what was going on. Running at the speed of a cheetah, I bounded over the side, turned the table, and vaulted over the back of the couch. Within seconds, I was on top of Tom, making weird grunting noises.

"What are you doing!" Tom exclaimed. All the cloudiness of his concussion had passed, and the man was looking at me with giant hazel eyes. It was impossible for him to hide his fright as he wrestled under me, pushing my gnashing teeth away from his throat.

"It won't be long now, little Wendigo. Just a little further. Use a little more force." Clasping its hands together, the Wendigo watched with contentment as I attempted to exsanguinate Tom right there on the floor. I didn't want to do it, but there was something inside that wouldn't let me stop. I felt trapped inside my own mind, watching through two sky-blue windows. Tom's struggles began to lessen as his eyes fluttered. He was losing the battle, and it was only a matter of minutes before I would have my dinner. My eyes were fixated on Tom, but in the far corner of my room, through the grate of the apartment, I could hear the soft, methodical rhythm of a hand drum, and seconds later, the floor was filled with a mist. There was a subtle hint of lavender and rose, and I knew Kasey had made her appearance.

The fog crept across the floor, covering Tom's body. It was making its way to the Wendigo, and the monster didn't like it.

"Who are you?" it hissed as it backed away from the fog. "No one wants you here, foul creature."

"Look who's talking." Kasey rebutted with a hint of laughter in her tone. "Who sent you?" The fog twisted around the monster's legs, tangling into the thick grey hair that coated its body. You could cut the tension with a knife, but still, all I could think about was eating Tom.

"Get off of me!" The Wendigo screamed as it tried to push the fog off of itself, but Kasey just laughed as she entered through the sockets of his eyes. Howling out in pain, the monster danced around the room drunkenly. It clawed at its face, leaving deep gashes in its skulled head. Rushing back towards the window, the monster growled, snatching a knife from the counter.

"What are you going to do with that?" Kasey said with amusement. "You can't kill me... But if you don't leave now, I might kill you." Sliding the blade through its socket, the Wendigo screamed and stomped across the broken glass on the floor. "WHO SENT YOU?" Kasey screamed.

"Sally... Sally Wells." Yanking back the knife, the monster huffed as the smoke began to clear from its body. It ran forward, taking one giant leap through the window.

The lights flickered on seconds later, and I stopped feeling so murdery. Letting go of Tom's arms, I rolled off of him, letting out a giant sigh of relief. Touching my teeth with my fingers, I noticed they were back to normal, and I didn't feel so trapped. Tom, on the other hand, had finally given up the good fight. His arms had gone limp, and his eyes had shut completely. He was out like a light, and with good reason. A large pool of blood had formed on the carpet beside him. The gash wouldn't close.

"Is it over?" I asked, covering my eyes with one of my arms. I could feel a headache coming on, and I hated getting them.

"I'm not sure," Kasey's disembodied voice replied. "I haven't had a lot of run-ins with Wendigos. They're a tricky bunch with a lot of lore about their curse."

"Is that how it got to me? Am I cursed now?" There was a long pause before the fog made its way towards us. The closer it got, the warmer the apartment became, and I knew that the monster was running for the hills. I could see tufts of reddish hair flowing in the breeze and realized that whatever special magic Kasey had used to get to us was beginning to wear off.

"If that's what it did, then you could relapse. I'll have to look up how to break the curse... You didn't bite him, did you?" Taking my arm away from my face, I looked at the sleeping man and shook my head.

"No, he's stronger than he looks." Leaning over him, I cradled his face in my hands and lowered my brow. "I'm pretty sure he needs a doctor, though. The Wendigo threw him against the wall pretty hard, and that cut on his head won't stop bleeding."

At this point, Kasey was almost back to her old self, but I could tell the smell of blood in the air was turning her stomach. She had a green hew to her already undead flesh, and it was a matter of moments before she blew chunks all over my apartment again.

"I should go back down to the basement... I have a guy who can fix Tom right up." As Kasey floated towards the door, she grabbed her stomach. Weird sounds were coming from deep within her, and I knew she was doing all she could to keep her composure. I didn't say another word. Turning my attention back to Tom, I looked into his face, waiting for his hazel eyes to open. The longer he laid there on the floor stationary, the more concerned I became. What if I had killed him? What if letting him tag along back at the General store led to his demise? My heart couldn't take it. He had to wake up... Right?

Chapter Seven
FETCH!

"There's something wrong with him!"

"There's nothing wrong with him. He's just a little different from the normal people I bring your way."

"No... There's definitely something wrong with this guy, and to be perfectly honest with you, I don't think I should treat him." Smita looked at the man in the blue hoodie and crossed her arms. She didn't have time for all the nonsense. It had been a long night, and now that the sun was coming up, she wanted to get back to normalcy... Or at least what passed for it here in the apartment complex.

Kasey had retired back into the basement, but not before ripping the door off its hinges. There was no way she was going to get caught in that room with Neith again... Not unprepared, that is. She had given Smita Doctor Reven's number and told her to tell the man that a friend had an accident. He was the only doctor who did house calls in town and owed Kasey a favor.

"Well then, what makes you think my friend over here is damaged goods?" Leaning against the wall, Doctor Reven straightened the bottle cap glasses on the bridge of his nose and sighed.

"Ms. Chatter, I know that you don't want to hear this right now, but there is a plethora of things wrong here. Just by your association with Kasey, I can assume that you know that there is more out there than mere humans roaming the streets. I'm just suggesting that Tom, over there, is one of those other... Things." Tapping her foot, Smita wrinkled her nose, thought about what the man had said for a second, and then laughed loudly.

"No, no, there's no way that Tom is anything other than human. He can't even whistle, for God's sake! I left him alone in the apartment with Birdie, and nothing happened." Looking around the room at the carnage and flipped over furniture, the man in the blue hoodie smirked a little and cocked his head.

"Yeah, it sure looked like nothing happened in here."

"No, you see, that was the Wendigo. It broke through the window and attacked them. That's why Tom's head is so messed up."

"A Wendigo, you say?" Reven asked as he walked towards Tom.

After Reven and Smita fixed my door, they had put Tom on my bed, but at that point, I had lost it completely. Smita suggested I stay out of the room until I was able to gather my wits, but hours had passed, and I still hadn't been able to wrap my head around everything that had happened. Even though I was sitting out on the living room couch, I could hear what they were saying. I didn't appreciate what Doctor Reven was implying, either. Tom was nothing more than a living, breathing, red-blooded American boy... At least, it looked that way to me.

Turning my attention to the open doorway, I gathered my courage and wandered to the room where the others were. Smita and Reven were hunched over the sleeping man, whispering back and forth between themselves.

"What's going on?" I asked as I inched closer to the action. Straightening up at my voice, Smita turned around and put on her best fake smile.

"It's nothing Birdie. Don't worry about it."

"Oh, I'm going to worry about it, Smita. I might be cursed, and now you two are talking like Tom has cooties or something." This time, it was Reven's turn to swing around with wide eyes and a shocked look on his face.

"Oh, my dear, don't mention cooties! What a horrible thing to say about someone." Slack-jawed, my eyes drifted from Smita to the man in the blue sweater. I had no words. "I need you to tell me exactly what happened last night. What happened after the Wendigo entered the house."

"What do you mean, 'what did it do?' The damn thing went after me. It shook Tom around like it was expecting candy to come out of him, and when he got bored with him, it came after me. It cursed me, and I almost ate my friend!" Pacing the floor, I scratched the top of my head and groaned. "You don't have a prescription? A pill or an ointment that cures curses, do you?"

Shaking his head, the man clicked his tongue on the roof of his mouth and adjusted his glasses again.

"No. That's more of Kasey's thing."

"I figured." Sitting in the middle of the floor, I grabbed the lamp I had thrown at the monster the night before and looked at the giant dent its goofy head had made in the metal. I couldn't help but worry that it would come back to finish the job... Or worse, have me finish the job for it.

"So you're telling me that this monster had Tom in its grasp and then let him go?"

"Well, I did distract him by throwing this lamp at his head. I figured he was just irritated."

Shaking his head again, Reven pointed at the little lamp and shifted his weight from one foot to the other.

"I don't think that's what happened at all. I think it couldn't curse Tom."

"Why do you think that?" Smita interjected.

"Because I believe your boy here's already been cursed." The thought of not being the only cursed person in the room was overwhelming. I didn't know whether to feel relief or concern. I couldn't quite figure out why the others were staring so intently until I realized I was laughing. It wasn't one of those 'oh how silly of me' laughs, either. It was the 'Go get the white coats and straight jackets' sort of laugh, and I could tell that Smita was more than a little concerned.

Grabbing the doctor's hand, Smita led him to the door and motioned for the kitchen.

"How about we leave these two alone for a little bit? I know it's all a lot to take in." Nodding in agreeance, Reven followed Smita out into the living room, mentioning something along the lines of a snack. Covering my mouth, I looked over at the man in my bed. I barely knew the guy, but I couldn't help but feel slightly responsible for what had happened last night. Swallowing down the last of my nervous giggles, I inched closer, trying to see what the other two had seen.

Tom didn't look cursed. He looked a little worse for wear, donning three rather nasty staples over his wound... But he didn't look cursed. There was blood all over his work shirt, and at some point during the struggle, the ugly white collared thing had been ripped almost completely open. I could see his chest rise and fall methodically as the rest of him laid limp on top of my favorite purple comforter. Letting my hand fall to my side, I walked closer, leaning over him, eyeballing his sleeping face. I had never noticed how the tips of his ears pointed slightly, and I could barely make out a sharper-than-normal K9 tooth that glistened in the overhead light. His lips parted slightly, and his breathing had become a little heavier... It almost looked like panting.

At this point, I was hunched over the man, inspecting the inside of his mouth like a deranged dentist. Was what Reven said true? Was Tom more than meets the eye? If so, it was our duty to keep him safe from Lupin Corp, and we couldn't just cut him loose like Smita wanted.

"What are you doing?" Tom asked groggily. Jumping back, I squeaked and covered my mouth with both hands as my eyes widened. I could feel the blood rushing to my cheeks.

Tom's eyes fluttered open as he managed to sit up. Touching the staples, the man winced and then smiled a bit, lifting an eyebrow in my direction. "Were you worried about me?" he asked. "You look like you might have been worried about me." Frowning, I dropped my hands from my face again and snorted.

"No! I just didn't want you to die in my bed. That's my favorite comforter." Shrugging his shoulders, Tom's smile widened.

"It'll take a little more than a baby crying corpse... Thing to kill me." Snuggling back against the pillows under him Tom looked away, glancing at the open door. "It's gone, right? After I fell out there in the living room, it all got a little fuzzy. What happened?" I could feel my cheeks burning again as I thought about jumping over the couch, trying to dig my sharp teeth into his soft, palpable flesh. I couldn't tell him I was trying to eat his face... I couldn't tell him about the Wendigo curse, at least not yet.

"Kasey got rid of it. You don't have to worry; it's gone. When you fell, you lost consciousness, and you were bleeding pretty badly. Smita called this doctor guy, but I don't know how reliable he is."

"What does that mean exactly?" Tom asked as he patted the corner of the bed. Walking over, I sat down and looked him in the eye.

"Well, for starters, he believes that cooties are a real thing."

"Who are we to judge? Until last night, I didn't think Wendigos were real, either. Live and learn, right?" Laughing, I pushed Tom's shoulder playfully. It was good to see that the man hadn't lost his sense of humor through all of this.

"Well then, explain this. Doctor Reven seems to think you're cursed."

"Oh, that one's easy. I am." The laughter stuck in my throat as I heard those words. It couldn't be true. How did we not see it? Clearing my throat, I took Tom's hand and inched a little closer to him.

"No, I don't think you heard me correctly. Reven thinks you've been cursed by something."

"Oh, no," Tom said in a low tone. "I wasn't cursed by something. It was Delilah. You know, the girl from the store? She rang you up. I was trying to tell you about it back at the van, but things kind of got away from us." Snapping my hand away, I jumped to my feet and backed towards the door. I didn't know what to do, but something in the back of my mind said to distance myself.

"You didn't think to lead with that little tidbit of info? What kind of curse are we talking about?" Shrugging his shoulders, Tom shifted his weight, throwing his legs from the bed and letting his feet nestle comfortably into the thick carpet.

"Thanks for taking off my shoes. It would have been weird waking up in bed with my boots still on."

"Tom! You didn't answer my question! What kind of curse are we talking about?" I could hear the others making their way back to the bedroom. Looking over my shoulder, Smita held a little plate of pizza rolls, and the doctor had a few bottles of water. Smita's laser vision was locked in on my panicked face, and I knew there was no hiding Tom's condition from her, not even if I wanted to.

Stopping in the doorway, Smita handed the pizza rolls to Reven and pointed a finger in Tom's direction.

"If you want my help... Sorry, if you want OUR help, your gonna have to come clean, Tom. You have to tell us everything... NOW."

Chapter Eight
Tom's Ex-Girlfriend.

"I had just moved here from Pensacola and didn't know anyone. Do you know how hard it is to move halfway across the country without a safety net?"

"You're getting off-topic, Tom. What brought you here today?" Wrinkling her nose, Smita stood in the doorway with her arms crossed. She looked more like an upset mother than a crime-fighting force of nature right now, but I couldn't fault her for the concern. Lupin Corp was clearly targeting us, and she wanted to make sure Tom wasn't a secret agent.

"Look, I just wanted to tell you everything, you know, like you told me to?" Rolling his eyes, Tom got to his feet and paced the floor for a second. "Aw, man, my shirt is ruined."

"Here," I said quickly. Rushing to the closet door, I slung it open and pulled out the first shirt I saw. It was an oversized pink tank top that said Moondust College on the front. Throwing it at

Tom, he caught it mid-flight and put it on without complaint. I figured the man didn't want to make any more waves than he already had... And to be honest, pink was his color.

"Okay, so you made it here from Florida and didn't know anyone... Then what happened?" Smita's irritation dripped from every word she spoke, and I didn't like it. Usually, my best friend had a good head on her shoulders, but the minute she felt jaded or made a fool of, she often flew off the handle and it was almost impossible to pull her back off that ledge. Tom didn't seem to notice, though, putting a finger in the air and sighing quietly.

"I took a job delivering drinks for the local soda company. A buddy from my old life back in Pensacola called in a favor. Everything was going well for a while until I met Delilah. I even scored a room with two dudes across town. I guess I find it odds now, seeing as she had just moved down here herself and had taken on the second shift position at the little store you frequented last night. Man, she was amazing... Beautiful and funny." I could see the man's eyes begin to glaze over as he thought back to the first day he had met Delilah. He had a faraway look and a crooked, drunklike expression on his face.

Snapping my fingers, I inched closer as he slowly came back to reality.

"The girl I met at the checkout last night? You thought she was beautiful... And funny?" Nodding quietly, Tom pushed the hair away from his face and scratched his chin.

"Yeah, she's pretty smart too." Turning my attention towards Reven, the doctor could tell I had questions.

"It's part of the curse. You see, Rougarou's often send out pheromones that attract potential mates... And meals." Snapping, Smita laughed loudly for a second and then poked Reven in the chest with her index finger.

"There's your proof right there, Doc. Tom isn't sending out any pheromones to me or Birdie. He's the same old skinny dork he's always been... Well, for as long as I've known him."

"No! I'm telling you, I'm cursed, and Delilah did it." Pointing a finger at a set of old scars on his shoulder, Tom lifted an eyebrow. "It happened two months ago. I was at her place, and we were..."

"Yeah, yeah, we can guess what you were doing," I said as I waved a hand in the man's face.

"Well," Tom continued, looking down at the ground, "there was more to our relationship than just that... But yes, I'm sure you can guess. The window to her bedroom was open, and the moonlight was shifting through the open glass. Before I knew it, she was turning into this bag nasty dog looking thing. I managed to get away, but not before she scratched me. I went to the hospital and told them what had happened, but then there was talk about a psych evaluation, so I just got out of there. After a few days, I had convinced myself that maybe I had imagined it all. You know that maybe Delilah had just gotten rough in bed, and I couldn't handle it or something. It was weird because the cuts on my arm healed up fast, but I wasn't complaining."

"That was until the next full moon, right?" Reven asked as he glanced back at Smita, who was anything but amused. "Do you remember what happened that night?"

Shaking his head, Tom sat down on the edge of the bed and crossed his arms over his chest.

"It's all a blur, but I woke up in my neighbor's yard, all covered in blood. Later that day, I heard that something had gotten into his chicken coop and ate all seventeen of his chickens."

"At least you didn't hurt anyone!" I exclaimed as I backed away from Tom, again pressing my shoulder against Smita's.

"Don't you think I know that!" Tom shot back. "That's why I started asking around. When Delilah stopped taking my calls, I had to figure out where else to go. I kept my distance when you were going after the Squonk. I snuck in the back when you went through the front. I found that name tag in the break room and stuck it on my shirt. It wasn't a coincidence meeting you at the general store, Birdie. I was there to ask for your help." Lowering my brow, I clicked my tongue against the roof of my mouth and pointed down to the discarded, ripped, and bloody shirt on the floor.

"So then... What's your real name?"

"Raphiel. My mom was an art major."

"You've been here all night, letting us call you Tom... Explain that." The heat in my voice concerned Raph more than the anger in Smita's and it was at that moment I realized that my opinion of him mattered more in his eyes than the woman who could possibly save him. My heart softened a bit, but I wouldn't let him know that. "Maybe you should go home and really think about all this. How can we trust you, knowing what we know now?" His stare intensified as he counted each fiber in the carpet. Nodding, he instinctively rubbed the scars he had pointed out earlier.

"You're right. I should have been more transparent from the beginning. I just didn't think you two would put me on a high-priority list if I didn't insert myself into something a little more important."

"Well, now, you can consider yourself at the bottom of our list. I wish I could say it was nice to meet you, but..." Even as I spoke, I could feel the sting of my own words. I didn't understand why I was so upset, but something inside me felt jilted, and it was more than just my ego.

Walking towards the door, Raphiel grabbed the plate of pizza rolls and began to pop them into his mouth.

"I'll see myself out." He mumbled. Smita watched as the man reached the door. Setting the empty plate on the table where I often left my keys, he grabbed the handle, but before he could open the door and leave our lives for good, Smita blurted out something I never thought I would hear her say.

"WAIT!" Turning around, Raph looked Smita in the eyes with confusion. "As much as it pains me to say this, we might need you."

"You don't know what you're saying." I began, but Smita glared at me, which instantly shut me up.

"This is the second official Rougarou I've ever met and the first one that's actually wanted to have a conversation with me. Who knows, he might be able to lead us to the one that bit Kasey."

"You... You didn't kill it that night?"

Putting her hands on her hips, Smita cocked her head to the side and blinked a few times.

"I was caught off guard and didn't have all my tools with me. I'm strong, but I'm not that strong. If we could get to the monster that bit Kasey, we might be able to reverse at least one of her maladies."

"What does that mean?" I asked.

"It means that since her transformation, she hasn't been able to feed, so the Rougarou curse hasn't officially been cemented into her DNA. I doubt Tom... I mean, Raphiel... has fed either." Glancing over at the man by the door, Reven lifted an eyebrow. "Chickens don't count."

"So what you're saying is I can eliminate this curse?" Raph asked with hope in his voice.

"I'm saying," Reven continued, "there's a possibility."

"That also explains why your pheromones haven't kicked in yet. You're not officially a cryptid." Smita chimed in. Rolling my eyes, I rubbed my temples and sighed heavily.

"It also means he's got to stay here... Doesn't it? We can't let him loose when he's this vulnerable." Nodding, Smita put a hand on my shoulder and squeezed it gently.

"I know it's a bit of an inconvenience, but we swore to help those who need it, and Raph needs our help." I knew the woman was right, but I couldn't help but feel a little more than upset.

"Fine," I muttered. "Tell me then, how is he supposed to help us find the flea-ridden mutt that bit Kasey?"

"I think I can answer that question," Reven said as he puffed out his chest. "You see, Rougarou's often hunt alone, leaving hundreds of miles between the next one... But in this case, it looks like it's started a pack right here on Moondust Island. Each wolf has a psychic link to its maker and the one before it and so on. As long as Raphiel is holding the curse, he should be able to lead us to Delilah, and she should be able to lead us to the Rougarou that bit our little Vegan Vampire in the basement."

"Yeah," Smita muttered, "What he said."

"So, this is our mission now? Forget the Squonk, forget the Wendigo? Did you two forget that I'm cursed as well?" Waving a hand in my direction, Smita kept her eyes on the man by the door.

"I'm sure Kasey will fix you right up tonight. I mean, you didn't fully activate the curse. Raph is still in one piece."

"Yeah!" Raph said with conviction, and then his posture changed as he really thought about what Smita had just said. "Wait... What?"

"It doesn't matter," I replied with gritted teeth. "Why don't you two get on finding this Delilah girl? I have a few things to jot down for my dissertation. It has to be published in a few weeks." Walking back through my bedroom door, I shut it and began to pick up all the things that had been knocked over. My laptop had been flipped and slid under the bed with the charger still attached. Following the cord, I put my hand on top of the little plastic computer and pulled it out. Holding my breath, I opened it and then grunted with irritation. The screen had been cracked, and one of the corners had broken completely off. There was no way I was going to be able to keep writing on it. Sitting on the floor, I placed the laptop beside me and hugged my knees up to my chest. I could hear the others talking about something, and then the door to the apartment opened, and they all left. No one bothered to check on me; in a way, I was relieved. I just didn't have it in me today. Being that close to Tom, or Raph, or whoever he was that day didn't sit well in the pit of my stomach.

I don't know how long I had been sitting there when the knocks started. Three small raps, then two more, followed by a long pause. I thought about ignoring them, but whoever was in the hallway outside my door seemed determined to get an answer.

'KNOCK, KNOCK, KNOCK... KNOCK, KNOCK...' Even so, I didn't want to answer. There was something inside me that felt beyond defeated. I wanted to go to sleep and never wake up.

"Hello?" A voice called from the hallway. "I know you're in there, Beatrice; I saw the others leave. Could you come to the door so we could talk?" Leaning forward on the floor, I listened to the voice intently. I didn't recognize it, and that was a pause for concern.

"Who's there?" I called from my room. Standing up slowly, I walked towards the open door and out into the living room. "I don't want any trouble."

"I don't want any trouble either. I spoke with your friend, Smita, last night in the basement. I was hoping Kasey could do me a favor, but she's being bullheaded. Your friend, on the other hand, seemed persuaded... I thought if I talked to you, you might be able to convince them it's the right thing to do." Stopping at the door, I put my hand on it, taking a deep breath. Whoever was on the other side smelled of saltwater and brine.

"What's your name?"

"Neith. There are things you need to know. Things Kasey's done that you're not aware of... She's the reason that... thing attacked you last night and the reason it's going to happen again, but I can stop it."

I opened the door and looked out into the hallway at the woman standing there. I gulped back a scream as I took her in.

She was a slight woman with yellow eyes and tentacles for hair. Her full, pouty lips were lost in a sea of grey, almost transparent skin that had been riddled with a network of blue veins. If I was really quiet, I could hear her two hearts beating in unison.

Neith had a quiet air about her, almost as if she thought I was seeing something other than a horrible monster in front of me, and she smelled almost as bad as she looked. Smiling slyly, Neith put her hand on the open door and pushed it open, brushing past me with the grace of a gazelle.

"Please," I said as I rolled my eyes and shut the door. "Do come in."

"Don't mind if I do." Neith purred. Sitting on the couch, the tentacled woman sniffed the air and wrinkled her nose. "I'm assuming it's the maid's day off. It smells like blood, wet dog, and... Pizza rolls?" Glancing down at the little white serving dish Raph had finished earlier, I smiled a little and then shook my head. Now wasn't the time for reminiscing.

"If you were here last night, you know what happened. I don't have time for games right now... What can you tell me about the Wendigo that attacked us? How do I stop it, and how do I break the curse."

Patting the seat beside her, Neith motioned for me to sit beside her.

"There's a lot of things you don't know. Your friends have been keeping you in the dark, and it's clear where Smita's loyalties lie. She left you here alone to help Kasey. Last time I checked, Kasey could take care of herself."

I lingered at the door momentarily and then decided to sit beside the sea creature. What she said was true, and for the first time in a long time, I was beginning to wonder what I was sticking around for.

"What can you tell me about the Wendigo?" I asked again. This time, the smile on Neith's face grew two sizes too big for her giant head.

"Dear, I can tell you everything."

Chapter Nine
Beware, the Board Meeting.

"Kasey had called in some favors. She had gotten some eyes and ears inside Lupin Corp when she thought Smita wasn't looking, and I suppose it worked for a while. There were janitors and security guards who had been hired for the newly resurrected sky rise that could pass for humans, but that's all they could do. She'd been waiting for her time to strike. Sally Wells had been on the woman's radar for years. Normally, she hid in the shadows, out of sight of the real action, and more times than not, she was continents away from where Lupin Corp did the really dirty stuff. I guess that's why Kasey lost her shit when the news dropped that Sally was flying in for this 'super important' board meeting. To top it off, it was happening under the cover of darkness, in the middle of the night. I'm sure one, if not more, of her co-conspirators pointed out the irony of it all. There had been whispers inside Lupin Corp that Kasey was still kicking around out there, and it was only a matter of time before she tried to take the company down once and for all." Leaning back into the couch, Neith closed her eyes and sighed quietly.

"What does this have to do with the Wendigo?" I snapped as I clapped my hands to get the woman's attention. Sneering, Neith's lips parted slightly, exposing two rows of sharp razor-like teeth. Her eyes squinted open as she glared in my direction.

"This has EVERYTHING to do with the attack. You just don't have the patience to hear it all." Crossing her legs and faking a yawn, Neith closed her eyes and leaned her head back, resting it on an oversized pillow top that had been sewn into the back of the couch. "Maybe you'd do better alone, seeing as teambuilding isn't your strong suit."

"No!" I protested, touching the woman's shoulder softly. "I'll be quiet. I'll listen." Seconds later, the woman was alert, smiling with the teeth of a great white shark.

"Even though there were protests that this meeting could be nothing more than a trap, Kasey armed herself with several spells and herbs and waltzed up to Lupin Corp like a boss. It wasn't hard to get inside because her informants were manning the entrance. Cloaking herself with some of that weird liquid, she turned into mist and listened from the hallway duct work as those stuffy suits got settled. Just like she had heard, they were all there. Davis, Sally... Even someone she never thought she would see again... Peter." At first, the name didn't mean anything to me. I had been sleepwalking through the morning, focusing on a million different things all at once. Neith had paused for effect, and that was all it took for me to make the connection.

"You don't mean... PETER Peter? Not Kasey's Peter?" I almost choked on my words as I felt a knot begin to slide up my esophagus.

"The one and only." Neith mused as he slithered further back into the cushions. I tried my best not to recoil as the tentacles on the top of her head began to rub themselves along the back of the soft, white cotton. How could she seem so confident when she looked like... That?

Thinking back to the night before, I remembered how I looked into the soulless face of the Wendigo, how its eye sockets said nothing and everything all at the same time.

'Am I going to be like that someday? If Kasey and Smita forget that I'm cursed, will all my skin fall off

my face, too?' Shaking my head a little, I held my composure and scooted a bit closer.

"I know what you're thinking," Neith said as another sly smile danced across her grey face.

"You do?" I asked as I glanced down at my lap. The last thing I needed right now was for the creepy mermaid to be a mind reader, too. Closing her eyes, she sighed and licked her bottom lip seductively.

"You're wondering what a cute young girl like me is doing all tied up in this mess. I can assure you, Ms. Bones, there's more sitting before you than a pretty face."

Wrinkling my nose, I tried not to laugh, but something slipped out of my mouth that sounded a little like a fart. Neith's smooth demeanor began to change as she shot the woman a sharp glare.

"Do you have something to say?" She hissed as the tentacles on the top of her head began to dance like pythons.

"No," I stuttered as I tried with all my might to relax. "I need to know what happened. I need to know what Lupin Corp knows... And how screwed we really are."

Lifting an eyebrow, Neith shrugged one shoulder and nodded.

"Fair enough. Just know, though, when I'm finished with this story, you've got to help me convince Kasey to undo what she started. It's a matter of life and death."

"I'll do what I can." Neith mulled my words over in her giant blob of a head and silently agreed.

"Fine. I know it took a lot for the woman to hold her composure, even if she was nothing more than a poof of pink smoke at the time. I watched her from the hallway, hovering over the office grate, listening to the hushed conversations in the conference room. It wasn't hard for me to find employment there at the Corporation. The more eye candy they had cleaning up the bathrooms, the more distracted the suits would be when Sally made business decisions they might not have liked otherwise. I got paid pretty handsomely to stand just out of earshot and make goo-goo eyes at Davis and the others. You know, Davis didn't much seem to care one way or the other about all the hot maids running around, but the others took the bait… Hook, line, and well, you know the rest."

"Even Peter?" I asked. I hadn't even realized that I had spoken until the words were out and floating around in the air like a stale fish.

Rolling her eyes, Neith grunted and allowed her bulbous head to rest on the almost as big pillow.

"I didn't notice." She purred.

I knew she had noticed. There was no way in hell someone so self-interested wouldn't have. She just didn't want to talk about Peter and what he may or may not have done during this important meeting. Knowing I wouldn't get a straight answer about anything else, I decided to change the subject to something a little less... Neith.

"What was the meeting about?" I whispered. I didn't know why I felt the need to do so, but something inside me didn't want to say it out loud. Who knew, there might be ears in places there shouldn't be.

"The meeting didn't go on as long as I would have liked, so I didn't get all the information, but there were whispers, little bird... Whispers of BIG things to come." Neith batted her eyes and leaned forward, inching closer and closer to where I sat. I couldn't help it. The closer she came, the more uncomfortable I was. "The other cryptids and things that roamed the halls of Lupin Corp helped me piece together what we think the meeting was going to be about. You see, about a week ago, a cargo ship docked in

Moondust Bay. It had two important boxes onboard. One of them had that little Wendigo."

"What was in the other?" I asked. I could feel my palms getting sweaty as the smile on Neith's face widened.

"I couldn't tell you for sure. Whatever it was, it had died a long time ago, and Sally, you know the one, well, she'd convinced Peter to take a stab at bringing it back."

"But... How?" I stammered.

"Well, he's a necromancer, so..."

"No... I mean, how did Sally convince Peter to betray Kasey? Weren't they in..."

"In love?" Neith asked and then belted out laughter that echoed through the house like a million windchimes knocking against a battered tin wall. "Oh my dear, for someone who's a self-professed Cryptid Ally, you don't know much about them, do you?"

"I haven't gotten that far into the book," I muttered, making Neith laugh harder.

"You don't need a book to learn about us, little bird. You have to LIVE with us, and I don't think that's something you're ready for... At least not yet. Necromancers give away their humanity. Peter has all but lost his sense of self, and as far as I know, there's only one person left in this world that gives him the tingles anymore... And it sure as hell ain't Kasey."

I thought about what Neith was saying and all the things I had heard along the way. If Peter wasn't in love with Kasey but helped her anyway, it stands to reason he did it for someone else... Maybe someone who's been around longer than anyone else... Sasha Shanea.

Chapter Ten
The Truth About Peter Nightingale

Before you learn about the man Kasey grew to know and love, you have to learn about the man he was BEFORE he was the man Kasey knew. I know that's a mouthful, but it was necessary to say so you could understand where this was all going.

Even though Peter Nightingale was a necromancer, proficient in his craft, he still had quite a bit of things to learn in his studies on the night Kasey Tomlin died the first time. You see, even though the people of Hollow Grove saw Kasey through childlike wonderment, calling her 'A frigging national treasure,' Peter still would have left her body right where it had fallen given half the chance. He had little interest in human emotions, seeing as he had begun to give them up, like a bad habit. It was a nasty little side effect of his craft, one he didn't think he would mind for the most part.

It wasn't untrue that, over the years, Peter had grown quite fond of Kasey. They spent many evenings sitting by the old book nook in her little house of plants and discussed their disjointed reality. She often had her fine plates and kettle sitting out with some tweaked version of hollencorn biscuits and green tea on display. At some point, she would pour herself a cup and offer a little to Peter, who almost always declined. Even though he had no squabble with the tea, he hadn't had a sweet tooth for biscuits of any kind in decades. He was absolutely sure that if there were any itch of humanity left in him, thinking back on those days might have brought a tear to his eye.

No, he surely would have left her dead on the floor that evening if it weren't for Sasha Shanea. While Peter had met Kasey a long time ago, Sasha had met her even longer than that, and even though she was born in the 1300s and in the original family of nightwalkers, her humanity was still firmly intact.

Sasha found her on the floor in front of the old nook. Someone had put poison in her kettle, and Kasey had done the rest. Sasha's heart would have been pounding if vampire's hearts had a beat that was. Her mind was reeling. She knew she couldn't let one of her kindest friends rot on the ground while she still had life left to give. It didn't take her long to call Peter, who owed her a favor or two, and he showed up, along with the elder council, within the hour.

"This is highly unorthodox." Elder Zanza exclaimed as he crossed his arms. He watched Sasha pace the floor between them and the dead woman. She was paler than normal, and that's saying something, seeing as she hadn't seen a sunrise in centuries.

"No!" She exclaimed as she pointed a finger in the old man's face. "YOUR UNORTHODOX!"

"Now now..." Peter began as he grabbed the woman's finger and pushed it down at her side. "There's no need for name-calling. I'm sure we can think of something if we put our heads together." Sasha knew that Peter was right and that cooler heads prevailed in the long run, but she hated her uncle and all the rules and regulations he felt the need to enforce. She knew that Zanza was one of the few original family members she had left but damned it if he wasn't old-fashioned.

"I think I have an idea," Sasha said as she tried to calm her anger. "It will only work if you agree to help me, Peter. Is that something you're willing to do?"

Pursing his lips, the man nodded quietly.

"That's why I'm here. I wouldn't have bothered otherwise."

"Good then," Sasha said with a smirk. "We can get started."

"If you're not going to take my advice, then why did you call me here tonight?" Zanza asked as he eyeballed his niece in the failing light of the little house.

"Because I may need your help too. It's something I've never seen done before. Hell, I don't know if it'll work at all, but we've got to try something. This woman's done more for our community than anyone I've ever known, and that's saying something."

Peter had never seen Sasha so passionate about anything in all his life. The way her dark brown hair swayed when she moved, her soft white skin almost shimmered under the yellow overhead as her amber eyes danced. He imagined a fire behind those eyes... Yes, there had to be a fire; that's why they were so bright and resilient. As her full red lips parted, he watched as she formed each syllable with elegance. Two semi-sharp K9 teeth almost the same shade as her skin played peek-a-boo behind them.

The night dwindled on, as most nights have a tendency to do, but that didn't stop the trio from bickering back and forth. Eventually, Sasha got her way, but you would have known that if you were paying attention at all. It took a lot more than a little blood and a lot of cemetery dirt to bring Kasey back to the land of the living, and she didn't come back the same. No, there were a few things that had changed drastically.

Zanza reluctantly took the kettle of poisoned tea back for the rest of the council to discuss who might have done such a horrendous thing, even though everyone else with eyeballs and a brain knew right away who was behind such matters.

Sasha told Peter that she would stay with Kasey until she woke and explained the situation at length to her. She also promised to make Peter look like a hero because if it weren't for him, the world would have been without its 'Friggin' National Treasure.'

At daybreak, Peter wandered out into the glowing sunrise and hitched a ride back to the country. He knew what he had done would seal his fate and diminish whatever humanity he had left. He had done many things with his powers over the years, but this was the first official 'Bringing the dead back from the veil' moment he had successfully completed. It was a warm morning, unseasonably so, but even basking in the glow of the morning's promise bore nothing more than mediocrity and boredom.

'*This is it.*' Peter thought as the paid driver left the city. Large, billowing fields of goldenrod and long-forgotten corn fields waved at him in the distance. '*This is the end of my humanity. I'll never feel loved again… I'll never feel accepted.*'

These thoughts might have seemed ironic to the outside viewer. Peter had accepted the gifts he was given and had taken into account the side effects. He even thought, for the longest of times, that ridding himself of human emotions would be more of a gift than a curse. Nothing had changed his mind over the decades, nothing at all… Until he met Sasha.

When Peter was a small boy, his parents had cared very little for him. His father was always away on some business or another, and his mother was a drunk. There was no point in sugarcoating the reality of it; that was simply what she was. Peter spent most of his childhood playing alone in the yard or in his room. On the odd occasion when his parents had guests, he would parallel-play with any children his age. Most of them didn't want to have anything to do with him either, seeing as he was never properly bathed, and his clothes were often worn down to rags.

As he grew, he ventured off further and further from his childhood home, and eventually, around his seventeenth birthday, he didn't feel the need to return. That was the last time he ever spoke to his mother or father. He did, however, go to each of their funerals not long after.

His mother was the first to go. Mary Belle Nightingale. She was born December 11th, 1740, and ironically died the same day in 1793. No one spoke about her cause of death. Even the county coroner simply said she stopped breathing in her sleep… But Peter knew. He knew she had drunk too much and probably choked on her own vomit. His father wouldn't have been there to roll her on her side like Peter always did, and he knew it was just a matter of time.

His father's death came just a few years after that. David Muller Nightingale. He was born in the summer, July 15th, 1736. It was on the day of his father's funeral Peter was approached by an older gentleman in a black cloak. It was hard to ignore the man because he was making no attempts to hide the fact; he was staring at Peter instead of the priest, who was executing the ceremony flawlessly.

"Can I help you?" Was all Peter could think to say, and the man snorted. Peter couldn't figure out if the noise he had heard was a laugh or a sound of contention.

"Are you Peter Samuel Nightingale?" the man asked. He didn't try to whisper, and his voice carried through the cemetery like a bad smell. The priest lowered his voice a little and fumbled over his next sentence as he shot the man in the black cloak a little demeaning stare.

"I am," Peter whispered back. "Whatever debts my father owed you, I assure you they died with him. I'm nothing more than a hired farmhand and have nothing to give." There it was again, that snort. Grabbing the boy by the wrist, the man in the black cloak dragged Peter away from the funeral and the prying eyes of the few people who bothered to attend.

"I'm not here to collect a debt, sir; I am here to offer you the life your parents never did." Peter's eyes widened as he looked the man up and down for the first time since he had spoken.

"I don't know what you mean." Peter stammered, but he thought, in the back of his mind, that he did indeed know what the man was going to offer.

There had been whispers in town about Brutis Barner. They had whispered about him in the dead of night while the lanterns danced low, lapping up the last bits of oil they had in their canteens. That kind of light does something to your shadows, making them long and eerie without intending to.

"He's here." They would say. "To collect another soul. I wonder who it'll be this time."

Peter often frequented the old watering hole where the whispers came in droves. He had been there the night before his father's death, and he figured, given half the chance, he would go there again tonight. He had an affection for spirits. He was a lot like his mother in that respect, but he made sure to stop before blacking out. The last thing he needed was someone to find him dead on the floor, drowning in last night's dinner.

Brutis Barner was the local witch. Peter knew it wasn't the correct term for what Brutis did, but up until that day, Peter had never heard of the term Necromancer. Until today, Peter had never laid eyes on Brutis either, but he knew who he was talking to.

"Where are you taking me?" Peter stammered again as he watched a black horse-drawn carriage approach with a driver wearing almost the same thing Brutis was.

"Into town. We have much to speak about. I'm sure by the end of our meeting, you'll come to see things my way." Brutis's voice was stern but not demanding, carrying an 'I know what I'm talking about' sense to it. Peter didn't say anything back and instead allowed him to be scooped up and whisked off into the midday air, stopping only at the local watering hole Peter would have ended up at anyway.

No one's sure what was said on the eve of David's funeral. Peter suggested they might have been in some kind of bubble, hidden from the view of prying eyes, and in the grand scheme of things, it didn't really matter. Come nightfall, Peter had come around to Brutis's way of thinking and not long after, they were back in the cemetery, but this time it was Peter's turn to retrieve a little something. Two souls. One was his mother's, and the other was his father's. If they had taken better care of themselves, taken fewer chances, and lived longer they wouldn't have been in the ground so young. Now their corpses were sitting in the dirt with unspent time… And Peter came to collect.

It wasn't the last time Peter Nightingale had stolen life from the dead… And every time he did, some of his humanity was left in return.

Chapter Eleven
Raphiel's Dilemma

Staggering up to his little single-level home, Raphiel fished around in his pockets for the front door keys and groaned. He had lost them somewhere between the general store and Birdie's apartment. Grabbing his throbbing head, Raph wiped away a tear that had slipped between his closed lids and balled his hands up into fists. Out of all the things the girls were in his mind, he never thought... Never in a million years, they wouldn't help him. Especially Beatrice.

Walking round to the back of the house, Raph grabbed the little wooden rocking chair sitting on the porch. He stopped by the window and placed the chair under it. He knew it wasn't safe, but he always unlocked a window for situations like this... Well not like THIS, but for situations where he had lost his keys. Stepping onto the seat of the chair, Raph took a moment to steady himself and then reached up and opened the window.

Someone had left the living room light on, but that didn't surprise him. He had two other roommates, and they were always doing dumb stuff like that. He gathered when the electric bill came, and it was higher than a stoner on spring break, they'd blame him, they always did. Grabbing the windowsill with both hands, he hoisted himself up and through the opening like a professional cat burglar. Maybe he was in a past life. He didn't know... he didn't know anything anymore.

Looking up at the wall clock, Raph wrinkled his nose and then looked around the house. Everyone was gone, but it was well after eleven, and they should have been home. The hairs on the back of his neck began to stand up. Something wasn't right. He thought back to the night before when the Wendigo attacked. It couldn't be that damned thing again, could it? No, the house was unseasonably warm, and the lights were firmly on. Not even a flicker could be detected from them.

Raph tried to calm himself as he made his way to the front of the house. It was a little two-bedroom, but Lester and Jordan didn't mind rooming together, which was more than fine with Raph. Being the nice guy he was, Raph offered to take the smaller room, and the other boys agreed. It had been that way ever since Raph moved to town, and it had gone well for a few months... That was until Dalilah came along.

"Hey guys! I'm sorry I bailed on our game last night. I had stuff to do in town. Jordan? Lester?" Pausing between the two bedroom doors, Raph held his breath and waited for the men to return his calls, but no one did. He thought about ignoring the cracked door beside his own and going on to bed without another thought on the matter... But he couldn't hold back his curiosity.

The light was on inside the boys' room. Raphiel couldn't see what was in there, but the little sliver cast a beam that lit up the wooden floor by his feet. Suddenly, Raph could feel a burst of rancid air as it pushed its way aggressively from somewhere nearby, making a pitstop inside his nose. The goosebumps on his arms only intensified as he hesitantly touched the back of the door. "Jordan? Lester?" Raphiel called meekly.

Everything flashed before his eyes. Everything was blurry but in high-definition and 4K all at once. He couldn't blink. He couldn't think. All he could do was stand there in the doorway of his friends' room and gawk in shock. The floor lamp that had sent a sliver of light through the crack in the door was knocked on its side. The bulb had cracked but hadn't wavered in its mission. The white shade had begun to burn, leaving a distinct odor of cooking cotton and floor polish. It was a nasty smell, but one that was easily overpowered by the smell of decaying flesh.

Jordan and Lester sat side by side on the floor, propped up by their beds. Cards were scattered about, glued to the floor by the boys' drying blood. They had been hacked and slashed by something ferocious. Everywhere he looked, there were four huge, thick claw marks. Whatever had done this had done it quickly and without hesitation... It almost looked as if they boys might have known their attacker. Something in Raph's throat caught tightly. If felt like a lump, but then it grew. Before he knew it, he was screaming at the top of his lungs as his hands balled into fists. What had he done? Wait? Had he done this? He couldn't remember if he had seen Jordan or Lester after the last full moon. Why would he have? They worked opposite hours. Had the boys taken the wrong night off? Were they home when he turned? When Raph got sick of playing with his roommates, did he go outside and rip apart all of his neighbor's chickens?

Covering his face with his hands, Raphiel stumbled back on his feet, almost falling to the floor, but he caught himself on the threshold and gulped in the air as his screams began to diminish.

'You have to get out of here.' He thought. *'If Smita, or worse, if Birdie finds out that you've killed innocent people, they'll never help you. You're a lost cause. They'll put you down like the rabid dog you are.'* Running into his room, the man slammed the door shut behind him and pulled a duffel bag from under the bed.

"What do you think you're doing?" A sly voice hissed from the corner. Screaming like a little girl, Raphiel fell hard on his butt and then scooted, pressing his back against his only means of escape.

Delilah stood in the shadowed corner. He could see her silhouette illuminated only by the cigarette she was puffing on.

"De… Delilah. How did you get in here?" He asked, but thought he knew the answer.

"You left your keys at the store." She said matter-of-factly. Walking towards him, the girl knelt and touched the man's face with smooth fingers. He could feel something inside of him twitch. Before all this Rougarou stuff, he would have thought it was butterflies, but now he wasn't so sure. "Why did you lie to those nice ladies, Raph? I didn't ghost you; you just didn't like what I had to say."

"Were you following me?!" Tom exclaimed as he inched further back against the door. He knew it was a stupid question. There was no way she was somehow inside the apartment with them or inside the van. Reven was right. Delilah had a connection to Raph now, whether he liked it or not. Smirking, Delilah took another puff of her smoke and sat down in front of the man, eyeballing him with contempt.

"You came to the general store last night to kill me if you couldn't convince the girls to do it for you. I'm not stupid. I know that." Snubbing the cigarette out on the hardwood floor, she smiled as the smell of cooked floor polish again entered Raph's nose. "You know that only works if you haven't killed anyone, right? It's not like in the movies. Once you've fed, your mine... And it looks like you had one hell of a dinner a few nights ago."

"How do I know it wasn't you?" Raph snapped back. "How do I know you didn't come here and kill my friends to get back at me."

Laughing, Delilah sighed and clapped her hands together.

"I'm not going to lie. It crossed my mind. It even sounds like something I would do, but as you can see, I was too late. So, I thought maybe you'd come around to my way of thinking... Or I'd just sit here and wait until you came home, have a smoke, and kill you myself." Something in the way Delilah said her words, pronouncing them with conviction and precision, Raph knew she wasn't telling him lies. It was at that moment he knew she COULDN'T lie to him. He'd smell it coming a mile away. It brought him both hope and sorrow. The connection worked both ways and if she couldn't lie to him, then he couldn't lie to her.

"Yes, it's true. I came to the store to talk to Birdie. I hoped there was a way to get this curse off my back. I didn't want to kill you, though, not if I didn't have to." Delilah's demeanor changed a little, and her shoulders softened. Her beautiful round lips parted a little in a genuine smile.

"That's sweet." She said. "I'm not sure if it's the part where you said you didn't want to kill me that I thought was the cutest or the part where you really think you could." Scooting back, the woman got to her feet, holding her hand down for the man to take. "I didn't mean for any of this to happen... But you have to understand I'll do anything to keep my identity a secret. I've moved all over the country... Someone, somewhere, always finds me out. That's going to be your life, too, Raph. It's a lonely one, but one we could maybe live together."

Raphiel thought about what she said and then thought about what Smita had said before he stormed out of the little restaurant by Highway nineteen.

"You're not worth saving, Raph! You weaseled your way into our van, hoping we'd fix you. You've got your problems, and we've got ours. Maybe this was a mistake. Maybe you should go home."

"You can't believe that. You're worth saving." Delilah's words were soft and comforting in Raphiel's ears. Her hand was dangling in midair. He could tell that she wanted him to take it. She wanted him to tell her that he understood her dilemma and he would run away with her that night. Raphiel wasn't delusional. Deep down, he wanted to more than anything... But he knew he couldn't.

"I can't." Raph began. "I can't just leave."

"What's holding you here?" Delilah hissed as she recoiled her hand. If Raphiel didn't know any better, he would have thought something had struck at her.

"What do you mean 'you can't?' Of course you can. What's keeping you here? Hope? Your friends are dead, Raph. As soon as the police show up, they will put it all together. You'll be on the most-wanted list in a matter of seconds. You can't just stick around." Leaning back, Delilah sniffed the air and then wrinkled her nose as if to say, 'I've only just now noticed the rotting corpses.' Putting her hands on her hips, the woman sneered and then stomped her foot. "Oh, I think I know what it is now... It's that Beatrice girl, isn't it? You've got a thing for her. Well, we'll see how far that relationship goes when you're ripping out her throat in a couple of weeks." Reaching down, Delilah grabbed Raphiel by the little pink Moondust College shirt and yanked him up off the floor. His eyes were wide with fear, but that only seemed to fuel the woman's rage. Screaming out in anger, Delilah threw him through the open doorway and into the hall. Falling onto his back, Raph slid a few inches before he stopped just under the bright overhead light.

"You don't understand!" Raphiel exclaimed as he lifted his arm over his head instinctively.

"Oh, I think I get it just fine." Delilah barked. Stomping up to the man on the floor, the woman reared back and kicked him in the gut with all the force she could muster. "I leave you alone for one fricking day, and you're already making goo-goo eyes at some hussy."

All the air had left Raphiel's lungs. He struggled to pull in oxygen. Everything burned like hellfire. His vision began to tunnel as Delilah bent over him. She glared coldly, placing her hands on her legs just above the knee.

"Just so you know, I was giving you an escape from all of this. I didn't mean to scratch you that night. I had mixed the days up... I thought I had another couple of days before the full moon. Sure, that one's on me... I don't know why I ever felt the need to help you; I know my maker didn't. He left me for dead in a ditch out in Cleveland."

"Wha... What... Brought..." Raph began, but he couldn't quite finish his sentence. Delilah had done quite a bit of damage, and he was sure there was a rib or two stabbing him in the lung.

"What brought me here?" she asked, looking towards the brightly lit kitchen. "I thought he could bring me some kind of closure, you know if I found the guy who did it. He left me in the dust, you know... There, one minute gone and the next. I followed him here to Moondust Island. It's the weirdest thing, though. I can't quite get a read on where he is. I don't think he came here on his own volition. Every time I link up with him, I see darkness... And he's hungry... Like REALLY hungry." Straightening up, Delilah pointed to the kitchen and stepped over Raphiel, who was still struggling to breath. "I'll be right back. I'm pretty sure I saw some beautiful silver knives back here. They should do the trick."

Raph wanted to ask what she meant by that, but he already knew. He had seen all the old-school werewolf movies and figured the same rules applied to Rougarous. She'd most likely go into the kitchen and find the housewarming gift his friend had given him in the second drawer by the sink. She'd pick the longest, sharpest blade and come back. If she were compassionate, she'd plunge it into his heart, giving him a quick and painless death, but something in his gut told him she'd make it hurt... Just like he had hurt her by not agreeing to run away with her earlier.

"You know." Delilah began as she opened the cabinets one by one, "I think, once I'm done here, I'll make a visit downtown, you know, see your little girlfriend for a while. She might like to know what you did to your housemates. I'll be sure not to leave out any details... Then I'll kill her too."

Rolling over onto his stomach, Raph ignored the searing pain in his gut. He didn't care if it was the last thing he did on this earth; he was going to make sure that Birdie was safe or die trying.

"You leave her alone," Raph whispered. He doubted the girl could hear him, but he didn't really care. The sentiment was there, and his intentions stayed the same.

"Ah, here they are," Delilah said as she pulled a giant cleaver from the second drawer. "I don't know why I didn't get this dang thing out earlier. You know, you plan on doing things, and then time just gets the better of you."

Grabbing the corner of the hallway table, Raphiel struggled to get to his feet, but he hadn't made it a step before Delilah emerged from the kitchen with the cleaver in hand. The warmth and compassion she once had in her eyes had vanished. What was on the other side of those eyes now was absolutely murderous. Her round lips parted, exposing her perfectly straight teeth. Running the tip of her tongue along the bottoms of them, she tapped the toe of her shoe on a loose board. "You know you don't lose your lust for human flesh once you return to your original form... You crave it all the time, like a drunk looking for his next beer or a smoker and their cigarettes. I bet you can feel it, too. I know you don't want to. You want to suppress that urge. Push it wayyyyyyy down in your gut." Delilah pushed on her flat stomach with her free hand and giggled. "It gets harder to ignore with time, Raph... And if I'd have let you live a year or two longer, I bet running away with me would have looked like heaven. Someone to spend all your time with that just... Gets it." There was no more talking. Lifting the cleaver over her head, Delilah charged with full intentions of lobbing off the poor man's head, and she would have too... If someone hadn't shot her through the open window, Raphiel had climbed through not twenty minutes earlier.

Raphiel watched with shock as Delilah stopped in her tracks. Dropping the cleaver, it spun around a few times before wedging itself, sharp side down in-between two neighboring floorboards. Blood began to form on her shirt from the gaping hole in her chest. She placed her hand over it and opened her mouth to speak, but nothing came out. Then she fell to her knees beside the knife, exposing the shooter to Raphiel's line of sight.

"Smita?" He asked. Raphiel had begun to regain his breath, but he wasn't sure she had heard him call to her. Either way, she climbed through the window and stomped through the house to the front door. Unlocking it, she allowed Doctor Reven to enter. Seconds later, he scooped up the now unmoving Delilah. She had passed out, face down on the floor, as a pool of blood formed underneath her. "Is she..." Raphiel began. Shaking her head, Smita slapped the man on the back.

"You did wonderful work, Tom... I mean Raphiel. We had to make you think we weren't going to help you. If you knew, she would have known, too."

He hadn't thought about it before, but now he knew what the woman said was true. She'd been so convincing at the diner, and his mind was on nothing else. Maybe Smita and Reven were on his side, but something told him Birdie was another story altogether.

"What happens now," Raphiel asked as he took a long overdue deep breath. "Someone killed my friends. Once the police catch wind of this, they'll think it was me. We've got a day, maybe two, before Lester's girlfriend comes back around. My money's on her finding them. Delilah's right about one thing. I can't stay here."

Nodding, Smita looked at the boy with a sullen face.

"I'm sorry to hear about your friends. You'll just have to stay with us until this all blows over, and in my experience, it almost always does. Until then, the mission stays the same. Stop Lupin Corp, fix Kasey, and get rid of these damned cannibalistic curses you and Birdie have such an affinity for."

Following Reven outside, Raph watched as he loaded Delilah into the back of a pristine white van. The old van with the back door ripped off was waiting for Smita and Raph.

"Where is he taking her?" He asked as he opened the passenger door.

"I could tell you, but then… Well, you know the rest of that saying."

Chapter Twelve
Pink Smoke and Heartless Folk

Long ago, I promised Smita I wouldn't go down to the basement of this apartment complex. Kasey had been down here all along, but back then, I was naive and just a little too trusting. Neith had told me a lot about what happened that night at Lupin Corp but left out what she called the 'juiciest' details for Kasey to fill in. I pondered on that for the rest of the day. Taking a nap around two or so. Of course, all I could dream about was that damned Wendigo and its skull face making my dreams less than desirable.

"Don't go down in the basement." Smita had said, pointing a finger toward me and raising an eyebrow, "there's vermin down there, and God knows when the landlord will call the exterminators." Those words had danced around in my head the entire time I stood inside the elevator, listening to it ding with every passing floor. Now, as the elevator door stood open, I looked down towards the end of the hall, counting the doorways I would have to pass to get to Kasey's room. She had taken the door off its hinges, and the glow lights illuminated the floor by the open doorway by a few feet. It wasn't enough to see every nook and cranny, but it was enough to make me pretty sure no one else was down there with us.

Taking a deep breath, I began my approach towards the open door. The closer I got, the more distinct Kasey's voice was becoming. She was talking to herself, trying to figure something out in her head that illuded her.

"Maybe a little more lavender... No, that's not going to do it." There was a little more mumbling as Kasey moved the glass around. I could hear it clinking together as she got her next amazing idea. "Where did I put those nettles... AH! There you are."

Stopping in the doorway, I stood there leaning against the threshold, watching the little vegan vampire work her magic. She was a little worse for wear. The blue veins under her black eyes bulged a little too far out and her skin, normally a beautiful porcelain white, had an odd sort of yellow ting to it. Whatever she had done to turn herself into smoke the night before had come to collect today.

Lifting my hand, I rapped along the outside wall, getting the woman's attention. It felt wrong being down here, even if Smita's banishment from the basement had been lifted. Honestly, though, I wasn't sure it had been.

"Hey," I said with a smile. Looking up from her little garden of herbs, Kasey gave me a halfhearted smile and waved me inside.

"I know it's getting late. I should have come up to talk to you earlier, but this whole Wendigo thing has me stumped."

What Kasey said caught me off guard. I figured the others had left without another thought about my newfound curse. Had they come down here and asked Kasey to look into a way to break it, or was she so intrigued by my condition that she dove into the conundrum herself? Either way, I was touched.

"That's not exactly why I came down here. I need to talk to you about something else." I spoke. I could feel my heart beginning to race. I hated confrontation, and this might turn into something of that sort.

Putting the herbs down, Kasey looked over at me, tapping her fingers along the brim of one of her glass jars. This one had sprigs of wild mint in it.

"I'm all ears." She said, but the enthusiasm had left her voice, and all that remained was a stiff monotone, one I didn't like one bit.

"I need you to tell me what happened at the board meeting. You know the one... At Lupin Corp?" There was a long pause, and then Kasey sighed.

"Fine. You might as well come in and make yourself at home. It's a bit of a long story." Finally, I allowed myself to enter the room. Walking carefully towards the hanging sheet in the corner, I took a seat on the folding chair by the little twin bed. Kasey opted to sit on the edge of the bed. Resting her head in her hands, the woman sighed again.

She looked tired. Did vampires sleep? I didn't know.

"You need to tell me what happened at the board meeting. I think whatever it was, it got me into this mess, and maybe it got some other people into it as well."

"I can tell you've been talking to Neith. I bet she came to you after the others left." Kasey was good at playing coy, but something in my gut told me that she had been listening the whole time through the grate that connected my apartment to the basement. Even though the vitamins she had been taking instead of blood had stunted her super strength and powers of persuasion, she still had sonar hearing.

"She stopped by for a while. We had a chat." I tried to sound more nonchalant about the whole thing, but a shiver went down my spine when I thought about the woman's enormous grey head and yellow eyes. Kasey's eyes glittered with amusement.

"You could see her true form, couldn't you? I figured the curse would do that. Most of them do." Rubbing her face with a free hand, Kasey closed her eyes and wrinkled her nose. "I guess I do owe you an explanation. It's not every day something like this happens… And I suppose I owe it to Neith as well… Even if she IS an insufferable little brat."

Leaning forward, I put my elbows on my knees and listened intently as Kasey started her story.

Kasey came to Lupin Corp on the night of the thirteenth. To the naked eye, one would have assumed she was there to collect her pound of flesh, so to speak. That was only part of the reason.

The night guard Mason Bruner had called her the night before, telling her about Sally's unscheduled arrival. He also spoke about the cargo ship and its two containers. While Mason was much less help than Neith and her little storytelling moment, Kasey knew that whatever had docked there a few nights prior had to be some big-ticket item.

"Are you sure you want to risk it?" Mason asked as he inched closer towards the wall at the entrance of Lupin Corp. Gripping the little burner in one hand Kasey frowned at the flip phone but decided to entertain her friend with a decisive answer.

"There's no way I can risk NOT going," Kasey muttered back. "Just make sure you're there to open the door when I arrive. I know you've heard the rumors, too. They're onto Smita. With or without knowledge of my existence, they'll be gunning for her next." Kasey's frown deepened as she sat down on the edge of her twin bed. "This was exactly what I was afraid of. I've been too close to the girls for too long, and now they've become targets." She didn't wait for the man to respond to her comment. Instead, she shut the phone and slipped it under her mattress with conviction.

Getting to her feet, she padded to the little grow nook and started pruning her garden. She would need all the weapons in her arsenal if she were going to pull this all off... And she only had twenty-four hours to get it all together. Briefly, she thought about telling Smita what kind of danger she was in but then thought better of it. There was no need, seeing as she could stop the wheels of destruction from turning further as long as Mason was there to hold the door open for her.

The day came and went, and Kasey worked tirelessly on the potions she would need to get in and out of the facility unnoticed. It wasn't until 10:30 that night that the phone under her mattress again distracted her. Rushing to it, she answered and listened to Mason's rushed information.

"She's here. Oh God, Kay, she's here, and she's brought someone with her." Wrinkling her nose, Kasey didn't know which to address first. Who had Sally brought? Why did it insight fear in Mason's heart... And why the HELL did he think it was okay to call her Kay? Did she look like a substitute English teacher or someone who sells insurance??? Certainly, she didn't look like one of those old ladies who worked upstairs in HR... I mean, what was HR anyway? Kasey had never been called 'Kay' in all her life... It reminded her of a single-letter response to a text message when you're angry at someone. Opening her mouth to say something in response, Kasey didn't get to address anything at all. All she heard on the other side of the line was Mason whimpering, and then the phone cut off.

Rushing to the door, the woman grabbed her bag of tricks and a light jacket and hailed a cab down the street from the apartment. Kasey hadn't worried about being seen that night because Smita and dragged Birdie across town to hunt a Squonk. Squonks were ferociously reclusive, and Kasey doubted the duo would return before sunrise. It hadn't dawned on her that someone could have been watching them as intently as Kasey had been watching Lupin Corp. She thought she had time before anything bad happened, and that was her first mistake.

"Stop here," Kasey said as she tapped her driver on the shoulder. Pulling over to the curb, the driver put the car in park as Kasey handed the man a twenty. "No need to wait for me. I have a ride home." Scoffing, the overweight, middle-aged man rolled his eyes and shifted the car into gear.

"I wouldn't have even if you'd asked. I've got shit to do, and you can wait for another car if you need one so bad." Stepping out onto the sidewalk, Kasey watched with irritation as the fat man made a half doughnut in his car, squalling tires, and vanished down High Street. It was the opposite direction in which she was going, and for some reason, it made her feel a little better.

"At least I won't have to worry about him blubbering about I guess." She said more to herself than anyone else who might have been in earshot at that moment. Adjusting her bag, Kasey made the short walk two blocks down to Lupin Corp's main office.

It didn't look like much, and most of the people on Moondust Island didn't give the small, unmarked building much thought, but Kasey knew what was on the inside. Even though most of Lupin Corp's experiments were done off-site, Kasey did not doubt that a few success stories were wandering down those halls, and she hoped she wouldn't happen across any of them before she finished what she had come there to do.

Keeping her head down, Kasey pulled her hair back into a messy bun and lifted the hood on the back of her sweater.

"Stop!" the first security officer said with authority. Kasey did as she was told but kept her head down so they couldn't get a look at her face or the two marble-shaped black eyes she was now sporting.

"I'm sorry. I didn't mean to startle anyone. My name is Alice, and I believe I'm a little lost." The officer scoffed and waved the woman away with a dismissive hand.

"I don't think you belong here, ma'am. If you're looking for the Moondust Hotel, it's two blocks over." Kasey stood there for a few moments before turning on her heels. Where the hell was Mason? He was supposed to let her in. Without his help, she'd be stuck out there. Making it back onto the sidewalk, Kasey sighed. She was about to pull her hood down when she heard something coming from the side gate.

"PSST." Turning her head slowly, the woman scoured the area, looking for the source of the sound. "PSST!" This time the noise was a little louder, with more definition. "Hey, Kay! I'm over here." Grunting under her breath, Kasey walked around the side of the building. Mason was on the other side of the chain link fencing.

"Why aren't you at your post?" Kasey demanded. Even though she was whispering, Mason could hear the scolding nature it entailed.

"I'm sorry!" Mason whimpered. "I tried to get there, but Orwell beat me to it. He's been gunning for the new Chief position, and I think he might actually get it."

"Well, good for him," Kasey said as she rolled her eyes. "Can you get me in?" Mason shrugged and then pointed to the back door.

"It's unlocked, but you'll have to climb this ten-foot wall."

Inching towards the chained gate door, Kasey put her bag down and pushed it through towards the man, but before she did, she took out a little vial that held a white liquid. To Mason, it looked like milk.

"Do me a favor and put my bag in the supply closet. I may need what's in there when I regain my senses." Popping the top from her little glass vial, Kasey downed the shot of 'milk,' and moments later, she was nothing more than a poof of pink smoke. Mason's eyes widened into half dollars as his mouth opened in awe.

"I'll never figure out how you do all that cool shit." Snatching up the bag, Mason followed the poof of smoke to the unlocked door and opened it. A few seconds later, Kasey had made herself at home inside the heating duct of the facility.

Slipping the bag into the nearest hall closet, Mason ran to the grate and pressed his face against it. "They're two rooms down. I think the meetings about to start... I don't know if I can help you get out without blowing my cover."

"You let me handle that part," Kasey said. Her voice echoed inside the metal piping, making her sound slightly louder than she would have liked. "You've done your part." She finished. She spoke a little quieter this time, so anyone with prying ears didn't hear.

Backing away from the grate, Mason nodded and took his cue. He knew he couldn't be away from his post for too long, or someone might see, and that was the last thing either of them wanted.

Following the sound of people talking, Kasey easily found the conference room Mason had spoken about. There were five people in the room. Three of them Kasey was expecting... Two of them she was not. The first person she saw was none other than Davis Kellerman. He looked the same as he had on the night of her abduction. Tall, but not too tall with a little bit of chub around the middle. His ambiguous face told the person looking at it he could be thirty... or fifty. Davis sat at the front of the table. He wore his standard white coat with a plastic protector covering his pen-lined breast pocket. One hand strummed the edge of the table while the other scratched at his receding hairline. The middle-aged man needed a haircut badly, and his stringy brown hair hung haphazardly over his wide-set blue eyes. Davis had always been a serious fellow, but tonight, he looked even more forlorn as he bit the bottom of his thin lip. There was a clipboard in front of him, and he seemed way more into whatever was on it than entertaining the people surrounding him.

The person sitting beside him was Sally Wells. Sally was a curvy older lady with crow's feet and boxed blond hair. She wore black eyeliner directly on her waterline and bright red lipstick that often got stuck in the folds of her lip wrinkles. Some say she was too old to wear that kind of makeup, but no one said it to her face. Sally preceded Davis by almost a decade as the CEO and President, but she chose to stay in the field, close to the action. No, Sally wanted her finger on the pulse of Lupin Corp.

Some say the woman was the sole reason for the Nanjoglobe Lupin Corp merger in 2005. Marcus Goodhope, Nanjoglobe's founder, wasn't one to share the limelight, but there was something about the woman he couldn't resist. It might have been her money or the way she carried herself... But it was probably some trade secrets, mostly involving a little serum Lupin

Corp had been working on for a while now called Aphiborden. She had promised the man results, and gave it to him in spades.

Marcus had tried to replicate a similar gene he dubbed MX1 inside a test subject known only as Thomas but scrapped the project when he found out that people were harder to program than robots and then focused more on the technological side of things. Marcus needed the regenerative aspects of Aphiborden, and Sally needed Marcus's scientists. It was a match made in heaven.

The last person Kasey knew, was going to be there was Sally's right-hand woman, Lavita Thorn. Lavita was a woman in her late twenties, but she'd done more in her short life than most do in a century. Merely laying eyes on the woman made Kasey's blood run cold. Where Smita and Birdie excelled in saving the lives of cryptids and monsters, Lavita excelled in making things... Messy. Lavita was a larger woman with broad shoulders and the arms of a lumberjack. Given half the chance, Kasey figured the woman could rip an old-school phonebook in half without breaking a sweat. If that wasn't bad enough, Lavita was well versed in magic marshal arts and dabbled in historical nonfiction. Yes, Lavita Thorn was a well-rounded woman of the world, and she was also venomous.

Lavita stood behind Sally with arms crossed over her flat chest. She wore a simple white button-down shirt with a collar. It looked to be a size or two too small for her, but she didn't seem to care. Her long red hair was pulled back in a tight braid, and that must have been too tight as well because she donned an expression that resembled a cross between smelling a wet fart and discomfort.

Not much was known about Lavita Thorn, only that she thought of Sally like a mother and hadn't left the old lady's side since July 16th of, 2005. That was the day Sally's son was murdered in the small town of Holly's Grove. Some say she took the young girl from a local waitress.

Sally had come to Holly's Grove with a child and was going to leave with one as well. Kasey figured that would explain the young lady's sudden appearance and felt quite sorry for the waitress of the withering town. Lupin Corp had all but killed most of the residents, leaving the stragglers of Holly's Grove horribly disfigured with mush for brains. None of the monsters that inhabited the town would retaliate. Hell, none of them knew how to say more than a word or two anymore, often killing and eating each other without remorse.

The other two in the room made her tense up a little. No, that smoke could really 'tense,' maybe that would have made her fog? In any case, she stared down from the grate and thought, if she had a face, she would be scowling right now. How could these two have switched up on her so fast? How could they have been so intent on bringing her back and now be sitting in the lion's den, willing to make a deal with the devil? Pressing even further through the grate, Kasey got as close as she could to the opening without slipping out.

Zanza stood in the corner by the door. Out of the two, he was the one who looked more than uncomfortable in the brightly lit room. Jasey figured that made sense. This was probably the most light the elder vampire had seen in centuries... Maybe even millennia. He hadn't changed much from the last time she had seen him, wearing his long robe, black on the outside and purple on the inside. Zanza sported his short, black hair combed back with far too much product, reminding Kasey of an oil spill. His pale face almost glowed under the harsh luminescence of the halogen lights, giving the man heavy shadows under his eyes. He looked sleep-deprived, hungry, and, most of all, concerned.

Peter on the other hand, looked less than amused at the accommodations. He sat on the other side of the large table, with his back towards the open office door. His fingers were laced together as if to say, 'Let's get this show on the road.' Peter had always been a handsome man with striking good looks. He had sharp features that, when he sat perfectly still, someone might have thought he was made from stone. Given the situation, that might not have been completely untrue. His humanity had to have been completely gone for him to be in bed with Davis and Sally.

It had been a while since Kasey had laid eyes on Peter. He had let his hair grow out a bit, and it sat on his shoulders, framing his narrow face. His large green eyes sparkled in the light, but they were a dull sort of sparkle that let people know he had better things to do with his time than to sit here in Lupin Corp and stare at an old lady and her entourage. He was also the first to speak.

"So, you're telling me you've finally found her?" Peter asked flatly. Kaey could see that he was tightening his laced fingers together as he spoke. It gave her hope that he might not have been there on his own volition.

"It took a little bit of work, but yes. We've managed to locate patient 374410. Or, as you like to call her, Sasha."

Stomping forward, Zanza pointed a finger at the old lady who had just spoken with venom in his eyes.

"You watch your mouth." He barked as his finger waggled between Peter and Sally. "That's my niece you're talking about." Growling with irritation, Lavita took a step closer to the man, but Sally lifted her arm and waved Lavita's advances away. Hunching back in the corner, her attack dog stopped obediently, but she didn't look thrilled about it. The rosiness in Sally's cheeks began to return as she sneered in Zanza's direction.

"However you choose to name her, she's been in the bunker for about a year now, and she might not be... Well, the same."

"But she's alive?" Peter asked. Kasey searched the man's eyes for any hint of emotion. She thought, just for a moment, that there might have been something there, but it faded almost as fast as it had appeared. It might not have been there at all. It might have been nothing more than Kasey's wishful thinking.

Nodding, Sally grabbed the clipboard from Davis and slid it across the table. That seemed to wake the man up from his nightmare.

"I don't know if this is the best idea... I don't know if we should be..." Staring over at Davis, Sally gave him a warning look, and the man whimpered a little. His thin mouth snapped shut, and he looked down at his hands. It was all he could do now, seeing as she had taken away his clipboard.

"We weren't sure that you're endeavors to bring that Tomlin girl back from the dead had been fruitful... But once Sasha decided to cooperate we did not doubt it was a success."

Scoffing, Zanza crossed his arms and paced the floor, eyeballing the open door. There was a maid in the hall listening intently, but he paid her no mind.

"Then there was that debacle with the Rougarou. We heard from across the ocean that you had managed to get her bit... What on earth did you think that would accomplish?" This time, Kasey was unsure if the rosiness in Sally's face was from amusement or embarrassment and decided it was the latter. Sasha might have disclosed Kasey's whereabouts but hadn't mentioned her Vampire status.

"We starved that damned thing until it could barely walk... We thought, just a taste of blood, and it would eat her whole. Hell, Zanza, you know what a wolf bite does to a vampire. Even if we had known she was of the nocturnal persuasion, we might have chose the Rougarou." Davis's voice trailed off as Sally grabbed the man's wrist.

"She would have been dead long ago if you three hadn't stepped in. She would have been out of my hair, and we might not be having this conversation... At least not to you, Zanza. That woman, Smita... Something and her counterpart... Was it, Burt?"

"Smita and Beatrice." Davis muttered.

"Well, whoever they are, we have plans to get rid of them. Smita managed to get into one of our bunkers and steal Kasey right out from under our noses. Ever since we haven't been able to get a good lead on where that damned vampire is."

"She might be dead for all we know. Before Smita hit me, I evaluated Kasey, and she couldn't synthesize blood anymore. If she can't feed, then she will eventually wither away and essentially die... At least that's what's happened to the other vampires we've worked with." Tightening her grip on Davis's arm, Sally shot the man another warning look. He knew he had said too much, which could be deadly in this kind of work.

"Don't worry," Peter interjected, giving Sally an ingenuine smile. It was fleeting and fake; anyone with half a brain knew it. "I don't need you to sugarcoat what you do here. You're making weapons. Itemizing the qualities of cryptids and giving them to people. You're fucking with natural evolution. It's none of my business, really, and I intended to keep out of it... But you two seemed to have other plans."

Letting go of Davis's arm, Sally leaned forward in her seat. There was something in the way the woman looked at Peter that Kasey didn't like. There was something behind those eyes, heavy and dark.

"That's not what we're doing here, Mr. Nightingale. That's what Marcus Goodhope was doing. Do you see him here?" Lifting an eyebrow, Peter looked around the room as if he hadn't noticed the others and then shrugged his shoulders.

"Then why do you keep taking our cryptids? What is it you're doing with them?"

The rosiness in Sally's cheeks began to diminish as she realized she had the upper hand.

"Power and glory and being feared by people who are weaker than you... That's a small-minded business if you ask me. Marcus was a bully, plain and simple."

"And you're not?" Sally laughed at the man's question. It was almost as if she thought he knew the answer already.

"Hardly." She muttered. "What if I told you you could have your niece back, Zanza? What if I told you... For a small price, you could have Sasha back in the fold... And don't think I've forgotten about you, Peter. What if I told you I've found a way to give you back your humanity? You could have all the power you've ever dreamed of and the love you never had as a child. All you two have to do is wake him up for us."

"You mean the one on the cargo ship?" Zanza asked. Kasey thought she saw the man shudder, and that made her blood run cold.

Nodding, Sally eyeballed the elder and ran her tongue over a wrinkly lip.

"So what do you say, boys? Do we have a deal?"

Suddenly, the grate began to feel a little cramped to Kasey. How long had she been in there? The serum she had drank shouldn't be wearing off already... Should it? Looking behind her, she eyeballed the way she had come and then realized that parts of her were coming back into focus. There was no way she would make it back through the vents before she was in full form.

"Shit, shit, shit... I can't get stuck in here." She whispered to herself. Holding her breath, Kasey could feel her shoulders beginning to press against the sides of the grate. She couldn't focus on what the others below her were saying. Everything was coming at her in waves. How was it possible that she's metabolized the drink so fast? Then it dawned on her. She had forgotten her vitamin D supplements. The evening had gotten away from her, and Kasey hadn't bothered to take her pills before leaving the apartment.

Pushing herself closer to the opening, she looked down on the group of men and women below her. There was nothing more Kasey could do. She would have to crash their party.

"I know it's a big ask." Sally continued. "You both would have to stay here, on-site, until the job is completed, but until then, you two can have anything your hearts desire. You'd be considered guests." As she spoke, her eyes began to dart to the grate above Peter's head. Something had begun to bang around in there, and Sally shuddered to think they had been infested with rats.

"Anything except for Sasha," Zanza mumbled.

"No, that could be arranged. Of course, she would be confined to this facility as well." Clasping her hands together, Sally's smile grew larger. "If that's what you want, I can have her here tomorrow. IF you say yes now." Again, the grate above Peter moved, only this time, it waggled and bent as something on the other side began to curse and moan. Snapping her fingers, Sally looked over her shoulder at Lavida, who nodded without saying a single word.

The large woman trodded over, using her beefy fingers to pull on the netting. Seconds later, the whole grating cover peeled off in Lavita's hand. Kasey didn't know what to do. She was face to face with one of the strongest women in the known world, and her body was essentially mush.

"Hi?" Was all the little black-eyed vampire could say before Lavita yanked her from her hiding spot. Screeching out in surprise, Kasey went flying across the room, Landing face down by the wall beside Zanza. The elder's mouth dropped open in surprise, but Kasey knew he couldn't have been taken too off guard. She'd

157

always been the rebellious type, and this was something she would have happily done on any other given day.

Standing up in anger, Sally hit the top of the table with a closed fist.

"I can't believe you did this!" She hissed as she pointed a finger in Zanza's direction. "Why would you sneak her in here? When I've promised you the world."

"You don't honestly think I had anything to do with this... This... Woman getting into your little clubhouse, do you?" Sneering down at Kasey, Zanza took a few upsetting steps away, closer to the door and the prying ears of the housekeeper, who could barely contain her excitement.

Turning her attention to Lavita, Sally nodded her head.

"Well, if you had nothing to do with it, then it had to be our little Necromancer. Peter, was this your doing?" Snorting, Peter kept his seat. It would seem that the man with the sharp features was far less surprised to see Kasey. Rolling his eyes, Peter shook his head and waved a nonchalant hand in Sally's direction.

Scrambling to her feet, Kasey shook off what little fog she had left and then grabbed the side of the conference counter. Pushing it away from

Sally and Peter, she managed to wedge Lavita between the wall and the wooden table.

"I'm not going to let you get away with this!" Kasey yelled. "Whoever's in that box, he needs to stay dead."

"Maybe you should have taken your own advice!" Davis screamed as he lept from his chair. Kasey looked the most surprised out of all the people in the room. Davis was a meek man with meek mannerisms, and what he was doing now was the actions of someone ferocious.

Stepping between Davis and Kasey, Sally put a firm but subtle hand on the man's chest.

"I think we all need to reevaluate this situation. I may have been foolish to think we could come to some kind of understanding."

Opening her mouth, Lavita looked like she was going to say something, but instead, a loud croaking sound emitted from deep within her throat. Placing her hands on the counter, she used her strong legs to leap into the air, freeing herself from the tight embrace of the conference table. Peter jumped from his seat almost simultaneously, but it wasn't quite fast enough. Before the men knew what was happening, Lavita had them each in a headlock. Peter under the right arm, and Zanza under the left. Kasey watched with fascination as they both struggled under the woman's massive weight. It was now or never. Bolting from the room, Kasey dashed down the hall as she heard Davis's voice boom after her.

"Guards! Kasey Tomlin is in the wind! She's gone down the east corridor." She could hear footsteps gaining on her as she managed to round the corner. The strap of her bag was hanging out of the closet Mason had put it in earlier. She didn't know if she had time... But there was no other option.

"There!" The first guard called as they rounded the same corner less than thirty seconds later. "She's got to be in there." Pointing to the utility closet, The two guards inched closer. The first one had a nightstick, and the other a metal flashlight. The door was cracked open, but all they could see on the inside was pitch darkness. Reaching out with a quivering hand, the second guard pushed the first one along.

"Well then, go get her!" he said with an unsteady voice.

Stopping in front of the closet, The first guard took a deep breath and placed a hand on the handle, pulling it open slowly.

"It'll be easier on everyone if you come on out now." He said, but that's all they remembered. Moments later, a blast of light cascaded from the small room, blasting the bumbling security officers against the wall and securing Kasey's escape.

Chapter Thirteen
Lupin Bore

Walking down the hallway of office 12, Davis held the same clipboard he had taken away from him at the meeting a week or so prior. He hadn't been thrilled with the way Sally had reacted to the unscheduled appearance of the illusive Kasey Tomlin, and he liked sicking the Wendigo on the girls even less. Sally was a rash woman who ruled Lupin Corp with an iron fist, and to be honest, it was getting rather... well... old.

The double doors at the end of the hall had been secured with two electronic locks. The first one was face recognition, and the second one was a fingerprint followed by a four-digit code. Sally and the scientists left over from Nanjoglobe never used the high-security room; that was, they never used it until HE came. Standing on the little blue X on the floor, Davis waited for the first scan and then put his thumb on the finger scanner while typing in his personal digits. Seconds later, the doors opened with a loud beep, and he was through them without hesitation.

There was some nervousness deep down in his gut about having someone so unique held just inside the thin walls of office 12. Something about it didn't seem right. It felt too informal, too low-class. Shivering a little, Davis listened for the doors as they closed with a hiss. It was at least ten degrees colder in this room, and for good reason. The last thing anyone wanted was to spread germs. This room had to stay sanitary at all costs. If HE was who Sally thought he was, then bringing him back through the veil was more than important; it was mandatory.

In the middle of the room stood a giant glass bubble, and inside it, nothing more than the burned-out carcass of a young man hung in limbo. A bright cobalt blue substance filled the bubble to the brim, and it reminded Davis of a weird twisted fishbowl, only the dead boy wasn't floating upside down at the top like he should be; instead, he was just kind of hanging out in the middle, staring at Davis with the only good eye he had left. The eye was blue, but not the same shade of blue as the liquid that surrounded him. Somehow it was even more intense and immersive, sucking Davis ever closer to the glass.

"Don't touch that!" Sally blurted out. It was all Davis could do to swallow down the scream of surprise that began to swell up in his throat. Turning around with irritation, the man painted a halfhearted smile for the CEO. "Sorry, I didn't mean to frighten you. I just hate it when people smudge the glass." Lavita stood behind Sally, flat-faced and emotionless. Davis couldn't help but look at the giant woman a little differently after her attack at the board meeting. He always thought Lavita was an odd bird, but her frog calls sealed any doubt he had.

Pulling a white cloth from her front pocket, Sally pushed past the man and wiped the bubble gently.

"I didn't touch it," Davis muttered.

"Doesn't matter. Someone left marks on it. Probably some scientist or other... Always trying to recreate him. They can't understand that someone as special as this guy can't be replicated." Turning her attention back to Davis, Sally scowled. "Speaking of... Have you managed to talk some sense into Peter? Without him, there's just no way to proceed."

Davis wasn't sure why he tightened his grip on the clipboard upon the mention of Peter Nightingale, but he did. He could feel the dull ache of wood pressing into his palm as it dug ever deeper into his flesh.

"The man refuses to help. We may have to wait him out. Nothing the scientists do in office 6 seem to suede him." Davis's answer didn't sit well with Sally. Flinching as she frowned, Davis thought she might put HIM in an 'office' if he didn't get her better results. Finally, her demeanor softened, and she put a gentle hand on the man's shoulder.

"Davis, dear, I know you're not totally on board with this project. I know that there were people involved with it... During its original inception, that didn't fare so well... But you've got to get back in there and try harder. There's got to be something Peter wants that we can barter with. Waiting him out isn't an option. How many souls is he living off of now? He's not going to wither and die for years, and even then... If he wants to be a cantankerous old poot, he may still say no."

Lavita grunted but didn't say much more. Davis wondered if the woman could speak at all, thinking back to the croaking noise that came out of her voice box a week before. Then, a thought came to him. It was a thought he didn't want to say out loud. It lingered on the tip of his tongue, aching to come out and crawl into Sally's ear. The thought was horrible and vicious and cold-blooded. He knew that if he made the thought a reality, it might mean the death of Peter. Would that be so bad? Without the Necromancer, HE wouldn't be able ot awaken without Sir. Nightingale, the man in the bubble, floating like a dead fish, would stay unanimated, and that might all be for the best. "Well," Sally finally said as she clapped her hands together. "Out with it. You look like you're trying to do long division without a calculator."

Davis hadn't noticed, but he must have been standing there slack-jawed for the better part of a minute. Sally looked tired and frustrated. It was now or never. Should he suggest the thing he was thinking?

"What... What about the Psychopomp?" Waving her hand away, Sally rolled her eyes and laughed a little.

"What about Muhish? We didn't even need him when we collected him... he was just." The woman's voice trailed off as she thought about what the man was saying, and a wry smile spread across her lips. It was the biggest smile Davis had ever seen on the woman, and he was afraid that her face might start to crack. "I think I see what you're saying now." She said in an oily tone that made Davis's skin crawl. "Make sure you talk it over with Muhish. See if he can persuade Peter to be more cooperative." Lifting a finger in the air, Sally waggled it a little to the left and then to the right. "Don't let the damned soul eater take all of Peter's life away! If Muhish kills him... You'll be next."

Davis couldn't help but shudder as he backed away from the woman.

"You don't expect ME to go down there and get him... Do you?" His eyes were as big as saucers, and suddenly, his mouth felt as dry as the Sahara Desert.

"Well, someone has to. If you don't want to go down there, get one of the others to do it. Either way, I want Muhish in office 6 with Peter by dinner time."

Brushing past the woman, Davis walked back to the double doors. Even though it couldn't have been more than 60 degrees inside the room, small beads of sweat began to pop up along his hairline. What had he done? Muhish hadn't been thought about in years. If he hadn't opened his mouth and said anything, the Psychopomp would still be rotting away in the basement... Confined to office 1.

Pressing his thumb against the pad and allowing himself to get scanned, Davis typed in his code and rushed out into the hallway. He must have stopped breathing for a moment because the second the door closed behind him, the man began to gulp in oxygen like it was going out of style.

"Mr. Kellerman?" A sweet voice called from down the hall. "Are you alright? Should I call for a doctor?" Touching his hand to his chest, the man shook his head and then glanced down the hallway. Meeting his gaze stood the prettiest girl he had ever seen.

Her cheeks were rosy, touched with a kiss of pink that blushed out onto her tiny nose. She barely stood five feet tall, and her childlike concern was refreshing in a building filled with monsters. Her hands were laced behind her. Taking a few steps closer, the woman's full lips parted as she said the man's name again. "Mr. Kellerman, can I at least take you to your room?" Smiling, the man nodded, allowing the woman to approach. Slipping one of her arms under his, she walked him slowly toward the door marked 'DAVIS KELLERMAN, CEO.'

"I'm sorry to have frightened you. Sometimes, I forget to eat and get a little light-headed." The man lied. Smiling, the woman laughed gently. It sounded like happiness and childhood memories all wrapped up in one. Whatever ailments the man had before going through the door began to wash away the closer he got to the lady.

"Well then, it's a good thing I got here when I did. I would have hated for you to be on the floor unconscious." Pushing the door open, she pointed to the couch in the corner of the room, and the man sat down. "Can I get you a bottle of water or something from the snack machine down on the first floor?" Shaking his head, Davis put the clipboard down beside him. Closing his eyes, he sighed deeply and laid his head back against the back of the couch.

"No, you've done too much already. You're a housekeeper, not a nurse."

"You don't know... I might be a nurse on my off time. I've been told I have a great bedside manner." Sliding the board across the couch, the woman sat down beside Davis and rubbed his shoulders.

"I bet they do," Davis replied with a little grin.

"I would hate to be in your shoes." She continued, "You've got so much stress on you as it is. Sally should be thanking you for spearheading this whole operation." Suddenly the man's eyes snapped open, as he eyeballed the beautiful young woman with reprose.

"What do you know about this operation?" He barked. Sitting up, his eyes darted to the woman.

"Nothing, really!" She replied as she recoiled her hands. "All I know is Sally's been looking for a way to bring back her son. She's looking for someone who can fix things... You know... Rewrite history?" Laughing, the man relaxed a bit and slouched back onto the couch, heavily closing his eyes.

"You can't rewrite history. You can't undo what's already been done. You also can't tell that damned woman anything. Hey, don't you work at the Moondust Office? I'm pretty sure I've seen you there." Davis waited for an answer, but none came. Opening his eyes, he glanced over to where the woman had been sitting. She was gone, and so was the clipboard.

Chapter Fourteen
Full Circle

"Are you sure that's where he is?" Smita asked as she paced the floor of the basement.

"As sure as I can be," Reven explained. Smita's arms were crossed tightly over her chest, and her expression was stern and unforgiving. Reven didn't like this side of the woman. He had only known her for a short while, but he could tell that she had no problem breaking the rules to get her way. "I don't know if putting those two in a room together was such a great idea. He's still linked to her, and after what we found in that house... I don't know if theres any fixing him." Nodding, Smita silently agreed.

"I hate to say it, but if he's going around killing innocent people, we'll have to stop him one way or another. I'm not in the business of hurting fellow cryptids, but a change of scenery might do the goofy wolf a bit of good."

"What were you thinking?" Reven asked as he looked through the two-way mirror.

"Maybe the Scottish isle... You know the one." Walking up to the man, Smita looked into the room as well, watching Raph sitting beside Delilah's prison, waiting for her to wake up.

For someone who had almost died at the hands of his maker, Raphiel seemed overly concerned about whether the woman lived or died. His brows furrowed as he leaned forward, placing his elbows on his knees. Covering his mouth with his fingers, Raph rested his head in his hands. Smita figured it was easy to forget what she had done because his wounds healed so quickly.

"I wish you would wake up." He whispered. He could feel his chin beginning to quiver. Raph couldn't justify the way he felt. He knew he shouldn't be so invested in a woman who, only hours before, attempted to stab him to death in his own home. If he hadn't known better, he would have blamed the deaths of his housemates on her as well, but it was well-established that she couldn't lie to him. She had been just as surprised to see them dead as Raph.

Late in the evening, Smita had driven them back to the apartment complex. Once there, they loaded the woman up into the elevator. Raph was certain she was taking them to see Kasey, but instead, they stopped two doors down. Fishing around in her pockets for the keys to the empty rooms, she managed to unlock the one labeled 'AUTHORIZED PERSONELLE ONLY' and push everyone through. In the middle sat a silver-lined cage. Smita dumped Delilah into it and locked it down tight.

"You stay here and let me know when she wakes up." There were a few folding chairs in the corner. Raph had taken one and placed it as close to the cage as he could stand. There was a full wall mirror on the far end of the room. When Smita and Reven left, Raphiel assumed they were looking at them through it. He had seen cop shows, and this wasn't his first rodeo.

"I took blood samples from Delilah and Raphiel on the ride over. I tested it against another sample I had in my bag. This Rougarou has been around a lot longer than either of us has. The strain is old and deadly. That's probably why Lupin Corp chose it." Looking over at the man, Smita's frown deepened.

"What does that mean for us?" She asked curiously.

"It means you may have to break your vow of not killing anyone. Smita, this monster is big, bad, and doesn't care who it destroys along the way. To be honest, if it's the wolf I'm thinking about, I'm not entirely sure how the company managed to get its hands on it... And if it's the same wolf that I'm thinking about, Lupin Corp would be stupid not to have reigned it back in if given the chance."

"Off-site?" Smita asked. Reven nodded at the question.

"I'll call in a few favors. Until then, see what you can get from those two... And find out where Birdie went."

"She's a big girl. She can handle herself." Smita muttered, but Reven could see hurt in the woman's eyes.

The sun had come up before they made it back to the apartment, and the first thing Smita did, after securing Delilah into her new home, was go upstairs to tell Birdie the good news. The only thing Smita found in the apartment was a note. It was cryptic and odd, written on an old wrinkled paper towel in black marker. The lettering looked rushed, but Smita knew it was Birdie's handwriting for sure.

"*Smita,*

I had to leave. We took the old yellow truck from the parking garage. I hope you don't mind. An old friend came through for us, and we couldn't wait for you anymore.

B."

"How did you get that cage down here?" Reven asked as he put a hand on the glass. His brows were low as if he were deep in thought.

His words felt foreign to her for a moment as she was brought back to the present. Shrugging her shoulders, a sly smile crossed her lips.

"That cage was meant for Kasey. I didn't know what I was going to get walking into Office 3. She was disoriented. I think the safety net was warranted, given the situation. It just happens to be a coincidence that Rougarous don't like silver either."

That was a good enough explanation for Reven. Huffing a little, the man walked across the room and retrieved the bag that was sitting on the floor by the door.

"Please, don't do anything rash until I've gotten back to you." Waving a hand in the doctor's direction, Smita kept her eyes firmly on the two wolves in the room beside hers.

"Don't you have some phone calls to make or something?" Without another word, the man left. A few moments later, Smita could make out the sound of the elevator as it made its rounds back up to the third floor.

Raphiel leaned in closer as the woman began to stir. She groaned a little and rolled over before placing her hand over her head.

"What happened?" She asked sleepily. Raphiel could barely contain his happiness as he watched with excitement. Delilah's eyes fluttered open, and her once calm demeanor quickly turned into rage as she leaped from the cage floor, grabbing the bars. Seconds later, she was back on the floor of the cage, screaming out in pain, grabbing at the palms of her hands.

"Delilah!" Raph exclaimed as he reached for his maker.

"Don't touch the bars!" She squeaked. "They're lined with silver. Even a drop of it can burn you." Recoiling, Raph slid back in his chair, uncertain of what to do next. "Who did this? Was it your little girlfriend out to get a little revenge?" Wrinkling her nose, Delilah lifted her head and growled.

"No! It wasn't her... She's not my girlfriend either!" Raphiel exclaimed defiantly.

"And yet you knew exactly who I was talking about, didn't you?" Raph didn't know what to say. His cheeks began to burn as he kept his eyes on the girl hunched over in the small cage. Her shoulders slumped down as she began to sob. "Can't you get me out of here?" She wailed. "I'll leave and never come back! I swear!"

"I... I can't. Not yet, at least. Look, I don't know if it's any consolation, but Smita, she's not going to hurt you. If she had plans to do that, you'd be dead already." Suddenly, the woman's head jolted up as she stared Raph directly in the eye.

"I demand you go get the key to this archaic prison of mine and let me out NOW!" Closing her fists, the woman punched the ground. The sound of bone hitting metal echoed throughout the room, making Raph cringe.

"Tell me what you know about the wolf that bit you," Raph asked with a calm rationale that Smita had never seen before.

"No." Delilah pouted as she turned her gaze away from the man and towards the two-way mirror. "I have no interest in telling you or your little girlfriend anything."

"Don't you want to try and get rid of this curse? Aren't you tired of running?" Laughing, the woman fell onto her back, kicking her feet up into the air.

"That train has left the station, and you know it. Even if you get to the Rougarou, even if you kill it, we're cursed. Our future was sealed when we drew first blood on an innocent. Face it, Raph. Were fucked." There was no hint of satire in the woman's tone, no scent of a lie. Again, the man's chin began to quiver, but only this time it was for himself and the dark and uncertain future he would have running from who he was... Who she had turned him into.

"It might be for you, but what about me? What if I didn't kill my friends, and my soul is still somewhere in here?" Pointing to his heart, Raphiel's eyes began to twinkle. "You said you didn't mean for this to happen. Prove it. Tell me about your maker."

This time, Delilah seemed to think it over a little more seriously. Licking her wounds for a second, she finally dropped her hands, sighed, and nodded.

"Fine." She agreed reluctantly. "But you have to promise me something." Perking up, Raph smiled wholeheartedly and nodded with enthusiasm.

"Anything! What is it?"

"I'll tell you all about Rhudis, but first, you've got to let me out of here, and second… When you fail to break the curse, you leave with me. Say goodbye to your human life and escape. We can go anywhere, but we can't stay here."

Pursing his lips, Raph silently agreed, and moments later, Smita was through the door, pushing the key into the lock.

"Don't get any smart ideas; the bullet I shot you with has a device inside. If I think for a second you're going to turn on us, all I have to do is push the button on my keychain, and it'll send ten thousand volts of electricity right to your heart. It won't kill you, but it'll hurt like hell and knock you on your ass for the better part of an hour." Crossing her arms, Delilah rolled her eyes and curled her lip.

"I don't have a reason to hurt either one of you. I'm going to get everything I came for... Plus, it's not nearly as fun ripping someone limb from limb when you're in human form." Looking down at her feet, Delilah thought for a moment and then smiled, "but it IS still fun."

Smita didn't have time for Delilah's bantering.

"Tell me about Rhudis." She said bluntly.

"Is she always like this?" Delilah asked as she looked over at Raph. The man just shrugged his shoulders, but the woman could see the faint hint of a smile hidden behind those hazel eyes of his.

"She's not exactly the life of the party if you know what I mean."

"I can always shut the door again and leave you in here until you're more cooperative." Smita snapped as she tightened her grip on the keys in her hand. Her thub was dangerously close to the little red remote button, and Delilah wasn't in the market for getting another zap.

"No, there is no need for all that." She began. Slipping past Smita, Delilah stood beside Raph and tapped her foot. "I'll tell you what you want to know. I mean, theres not a whole lot to tell anyway. I didn't know the man long... But long enough to know he wasn't like other wolves."

"How so?" Raph asked, with a little concern in his eyes.

"He fancied himself a Vegan. He didn't like the taste of meat and flat-out refused to eat it... Unless he was in his Rougarou state, that is. I didn't know he had an actual food allergy until way later."

Scratching her head, Smita leaned in and looked into the woman's deep brown eyes.

"Do you have it, too?" Biting her lower lip, Delilah shook her head.

"No. I lucked out. It didn't spread to me. I looked into it, and it would seem that the blood allergy Rhudis has is only activated if he bites someone... Inhuman."

"So that's why it affected Kasey!" Raph exclaimed as he snapped his fingers. Standing up, he put an arm around Delilah and planted a gentle kiss on her cheek.

"Please," Delilah said as she began to blush. "What would your girlfriend think?"

"For the last time, she's not my girlfriend. At this point in the game, I highly doubt she even wants to talk to me... Speaking of... Where's Birdie anyway?"

"I... I don't know. Wherever she is, I'm pretty sure Kasey's with her." Smita replied. Her voice was heavy and tired. For the first time since Raph had met the woman, he could see dark circles forming under her eyes. Matching luggage.

"The sun is out, isn't it?" Raph managed to ask. Letting his arm drop to his side, his attention shifted from Delilah to Smita and the fact that Beatrice was out there alone. It wasn't lost on Delilah, and she didn't like it... Not one bit.

"Kasey is more than capable of traveling in the daytime with a little assistance. I'm not worried about that. I'm more worried about where they're going. Kasey isn't exactly known for her subtle attributes. If they think they're doing the right thing, Kasey will kick down the door of Lupin Corp and shake down the whole facility. I would say we should go after her, but I'm not sure which office they'd be heading to." Reaching into her pocket, Smita unwadded the crude note. She handed it to Raphiel and waited for him to respond.

"They took a vehicle." Raph said slowly, "So they must be going out further than Office 14."

"Office 14?" Smita asked, a little confused.

"I can't believe you've been fighting his company and never noticed those big ugly numbers on the front of the buildings. They're kind of hard to miss. They look fancy, but... Like... TOO fancy? Is that a thing?" Looking at Delilah for help, she simply shrugged and giggled softly. Then, something changed in her eye; it was a look of deep thought and then revelation.

"Hey!" She exclaimed with excitement. "I never thought of it before, but Rhudis had a tattoo... At least, at the time, I thought it was a tattoo. He didn't like to show it off, which I thought was odd, seeing as it was fresh. It was all scabby and gross. We were staying in a hotel right outside of Lummix. He'd vanished for two weeks on me... Radio silence. The older wolves they can shroud their thoughts from underlings. I didn't know that until Lummix. I had to go through the change alone that month, and it kind of freaked me out. When he showed back up at the hotel, he was... Different. He kept looking over his shoulder like someone was after him. I didn't care, though; I was more concerned about my own feelings. We fought, and he left, but before he did, he took a shower, and that's when I saw it. A tattoo, or a branding of some kind, all twirly in that TOO fancy sort of way."

"What was it?" Smita asked as she drew closer.

"A number. Like the one on the old building in the middle of town."

"What number was it?" Raph asked in a huff. Rolling her eyes again, Delilah kicked some dust that was on the floor by her feet.

"If I tell you, then can I come with you? I would really like to get a little closure on all of this." Looking over at Smita, Raph's eyes widened a little in a plea that would put a puppy's begging to shame.

"Fine," Smita said with a groan. "You can come with us, but you've got to listen to what we say. Do I make myself clear?" Nodding, Delilah covered her mouth with a soft hand. Smita could tell that the woman was pleased with herself.

"Crystal." She replied. "It was number 6. The number on his shoulder."

"Are you sure?" Raph asked. Turning her head towards the man, Delilah frowned.

"Duh, Raph. I might be a little emotional, but my brain hasn't turned to mush."

"Do we know where office 6 is?" Smita asked as she looked at Raph as well. Her emotions weren't nearly as angry as Delilah's. The man nodded and grabbed Delilah's hand. The girl softened at his touch.

"I passed it coming here; it's about thirty miles away and a fairie ride to the mainland. We won't get there until dusk." Groaning, Smita threw up her hands and walked out of the room without another word. "Pack your bags," Raph said with a smile. "I smell a road trip."

Chapter Fifteen
While You Were Out

It didn't take a lot of persuasion to get Kasey up to my apartment. She had told me about the meeting at Lupin Corp and what happened soon after. What Kasey neglected to tell me was why Neith was so keen on her helping someone escape. Kasey wouldn't utter the name of the person. It was almost as if she were frightened to; like if she said his name, he would appear and put a pox on our home. I didn't want to let on, but her behavior baffled and alarmed me.

We talked most of the day about the Wendigo and what she had learned about the curse. Everything she had tried seemed to lead her down the same road. There was no cure for the Wendigo curse. Just like there had been no real cure for her blood allergy, even if we found the monster, I couldn't be returned to my former self unless I killed it on the spot. Even though I hated what it had done, I also felt sorry for it. The Wendigo hadn't always been a man-eating horror show. It used to be a human just like me and that made me question if I could do what was asked.

"Would you like any more tea?" I asked as I walked back towards the kitchen. Between conversations, Kasey and I had tidied up a bit, but the blood stain on the floor by my door just wouldn't come up. Even though I had put a towel down over it, every so often, I could see Kasey's nose curl up in disgust as she sniffed the air, catching a hint of the coppery aroma.

"No, I'm good. I only needed enough for my pills." She called back. Nodding I made my way to the kitchen sink and placed the cups into it. The sun was already setting, and we had come no closer to a solution than we had the night before. It didn't help matters that Smita hadn't bothered to call the apartment. The phone hadn't rang once, and the mere thought of what she was doing out there in the real world only infuriated me more.

Kasey had been living with this affliction for a few years now, and it hadn't slowed her down. She could still feed without struggling... Sure, it put a damper on her ability to shift without a magic potion or two and she couldn't glamour anyone. Okay, okay, and her strength wasn't at a hundred percent either, but she was still living without too much trouble. Why did Smita drop everything to run to Kasey's aid? I was the one struggling. Didn't she know if that thing came back, I could kill everyone around me? There wasn't a magic potion to stop that!

Staring out of the broken window, I watched the sun setting behind the Inky Bridge, marveling at its beauty. Everything was cast in a brilliant array of pinks and oranges. A few moments later, I could feel a pang of guilt rising in the pit of my stomach. How long had it been since Kasey had been able to look out across the sea and watch the sun falter behind the old work bridge? How many years had she spent in the dark? Some of those years, she was painfully alone, and still she helped people whenever they needed it. I knew I was being selfish about Smita and her desire to help Kasey, but it still didn't sting any less.

Suddenly, there was a knock at the door, and it brought me back to reality. I could hear Kasey shift from her spot on the couch and shuffle to the apartment door. As I popped my head through the kitchen doorway, I watched as Kasey eyeballed whoever it was through the peephole.

"Who is it?" I asked. "Did Smita forget her keys?" Looking over her shoulder, Kasey frowned and shook her head.

"We aren't that lucky." Grabbing the handle, Kasey unlocked the door and opened it with a huff. "I don't know what game you're playing now, woman, but the answer is still no."

Smirking, Neith held a clipboard close to her chest and pushed past Kasey who was miles away from amused with the Siren's antics.

"I don't know. After my day, you might want to listen to what I have to say."

"Oh! Let me guess!" Kasey responded as she clapped her hands together in mock excitement. "Are you going to tell us you're running away and never coming back?" Twirling around on her heels, Neith sneered but kept her composure.

"Not exactly." She said as her voice lingered in the room, soft and sultry with just a hint of melody to it.

If I hadn't been privy to the woman's real form, I could see why men would flock to her. Closing my eyes, I could imagine a drop-dead gorgeous woman saying those words. Every sound she said dripped with temptation. I was lost only for a moment as Kasey's voice interrupted my fantasy.

"Then we don't have anything to discuss."

"You don't even want to hear what I found out? It could do you all some good."

"Not if it means I have to wake that sleeping beast! You don't know what kind of carnage he'd bring down on the world." Tightening her grip on the door handle, Kasey pointed towards the exit and stomped her foot.

"After all this time, you still don't trust me," Neith pouted.

"All this time, and you're still a spoiled brat!" Kasey snapped back. "You locked us in the basement because you didn't get your way, and now Birdie is trapped in a curse we can't lift." Lifting her head up in the air, Neith laughed silently and then looked Kasey in the eye.

"What could you have done to stop the Wendigo curse? Upstairs, downstairs, it didn't really matter. She was going to accept it either way."

"What do you mean 'accept' it?" I asked as I walked out into the living room. "I didn't ask for this curse." Turning around on her heels again, Neith eyeballed me in a way that said, *'I'd rather eat you than speak to you.'* But knowing Neith, I hadn't the foggiest idea which 'devour' the woman craved.

"I don't have enough time to explain your own affliction to you. I honestly thought you would have done your own research by now. Instead, I find you upstairs drinking tea like a bunch of old fogeys. I would have expected as much from this do-gooder over here, but B, you have so much life left to live. What are you twenty-three? Twenty-four?" I didn't want to tell Neith how close she had come to my actual age, so I stood there still as a statue and allowed the banter to continue.

"I don't know what else you can to do to convince me to help you. He's where he needs to be at the moment."

"Is that so?" Neith asked as she handed the clipboard over to Kasey. Reluctantly, the woman took it and began to read. Seconds later, she shut the door and pointed to the couch.

"Maybe we do need to talk." She muttered.

After a few awkward minutes, all three of us sat in the living room. The girls were on the couch, and I opted for the chair in the corner. Something told me that my presence was nothing more than a formality. Finally, Kasey broke the silence.

"Where did you get all of this?" She asked as she flipped through the pages.

"Davis Kellerman is a pretty easy man to persuade when you look like me." Turning her attention away from the papers, Kasey looked Neith up and down and then smirked.

"So you stole it."

"Pretty much." Even though the two girls fought back and forth like wild dogs most of the time, there was a comradery there that was undeniable. I didn't want to presume to know their whole back story, but something told me they would be bored and most likely saddened if they didn't see each other occasionally.

"There are lists here." Kasey continued. "Where all the locations are, who's in them, and what they want to do." Nodding, Neith scooted closer, flipped a page, and pointed halfway down.

"There's where you want to go. All the big bads are in Office 12." Looking over at me, Neith smirked. "Even you're precious, Wendigo."

"Okay, but that won't do us any good without a plan. We can't just walk in and say, 'Hello there, Mr. Wendigo.'" Suddenly, Kasey stopped me as she put a finger in the air.

"His name would be Steve. Remember? Tom called him Steve." Rolling my eyes, I sighed at Kasey's amusement.

"Fine," I clamored. "That doesn't stop the fact that I'm right about needing a plan. What are we supposed to do once we get in there?" I couldn't help but feel even more angry at Smita. If she were here, she would know exactly how to handle this. All I could do was finish reading the book she had given me on the Cryptids she had met and possibly find a weakness in their armor. I wasn't a fighter; without Kasey fully restored, she wasn't one either... Not really.

Leaning back on the couch, Neith sighed and rubbed her little grey fingers across the bridge of her nose.

"Unlike the two of you, I spent the better part of the day doing a little digging of my own. You see, Davis doesn't like to commit things to memory, or so I'm assuming, because he put all of his passwords and key code info on the back of the clipboard. I went to Office 6 and logged into the server. There were specs in there I hadn't even dreamed of." Leaning forward, Neith rubbed her hands together. It reminded me of a praying mantis preparing to rip the head off of its mate. "Sally wasn't lying about all the things she could do. She can give Peter back his humanity. She can restore Sasha back to her former glory... And with a little footwork, I believe we can stop this curse you've collected so carelessly from coming into full form."

"I don't think I can kill... Steve." I muttered as I rested my elbows on my knees. Leaning forward, I searched the Siren's face for answers.

"That's not what I'm saying at all. Nope, in fact, what I'm saying is the opposite. If we can get to the Wendigo, we might be able to bring back his humanity, too. We just need to flush out all that shit inside... You know, the stuff that weighs him down and keeps him in that form all the time. According to his records, he's old... Like one of the oldest living Wendigos out there. Chances are, whoever turned him is long gone. He doesn't have a trigger anymore, but killing and consuming is all he knows."

"That doesn't make any sense." I began, but before I had a chance to elaborate, Kasey put a hand in the air.

"No, that makes perfect sense... But how do we deflate the curse? We'd need something even bigger and badder than him to do it. I don't think Peter would be able to hold that much power... And I don't know if he'd be down to help us. I think he's switched sides."

"I don't think that at all." Neith purred. "I think he's there for Sasha. Even though he's lost his ability to love, those memories remain. I think he thought he was doing what was right at the time... Not to mention, you've gotten both him and Zanza locked up. They're probably in Office 6, and Davis dropped the solution right in my lap. At some point today, Mr. Kellerman is going to Office 3 to retrieve one of the rejected Cryptids. It was deemed too volatile to command."

"What is it?" I asked with a shiver. Looking over at me, all amusement leaving her face.

"It's a Psychopomp. His name is Muhish." Scooting away, Kasey's eyes widened as she shook her head.

"No! There's no way we're messing with that!"

"What's a... Psychopomp?" I asked. This time, Kasey met my blue eyes with her worried black ones.

"It's death, love. It's the pure, uncut, unadulterated end." I didn't know how to take what I was hearing. Death was a Cryptid? How could that even be, and if it was, how could we use it to our advantage?

"What you haven't bothered to include is that Muhish isn't here to take all the lives he wants. Psychopomps are bound by a strict code of ethics. They only take the souls that need to be taken." Glancing in Neith's direction, I lifted an eyebrow in confusion.

"What does that mean?" I asked as I wrang my hands together. I didn't even realize I had begun to do it until Neith pointed down and tilted her bulbous head.

"Nervous?" She asked.

"No!" I snapped as I forced my hands down to my sides. "I'm just trying to understand what you two are talking about is all."

"We're not talking about anything anymore," Kasey exclaimed as she jumped from her seat. "I don't want to be anywhere near something so unpredictable." Crossing her arms, Neith looked disappointed.

"For someone who's supposed to be immortal, you sure are afraid of a little death." She mused.

"I think I understand why," I interjected. My blue eyes twinkled under the overhead lights with fascination. "You've died before. That part is a fact." Pointing my finger in Kasey's direction, it was my time to smirk a bit. I didn't want to take pleasure in the vampire's fear, but I couldn't help it. Sometimes, it was nice to see that the things that go bump in the night also had things that go bump in the night.

"Yeah, so, what does that have to do with anything?" Kasey began, but her unease was as easy to see as a flashing red light.

"Do you know this... This Psychopomp? Is he the one that took your soul the first time? You know, before Peter jammed it back into your body and Sasha made it all but impossible for anyone to kill you again... I mean, without a hell of an effort." Neith's eyes widened as realization began to set in. I figured she had never really thought about her friend's resurrection and what it might have meant for the one crossing her over.

"Is this true?" Neith whispered. Kasey shifted her weight uncomfortably as her hair fell vibrantly over her left shoulder.

"I didn't think it was going to be a big deal. He never came for me. I thought... I thought he had other things to do. Now you're telling me he's been locked down in an office somewhere stewing in his anger... Plotting his revenge. I'm among the only humans he's ever lost in the fray. I can still hear him screaming as I was ripped from perdition. He swore he'd come back for me. He swore he would make it right."

"Does Peter know?" I asked.

"Does Peter know what?" Neith asked.

"That all the souls he's been collecting he's stealing from the reapers. All this time, the man's been picking death's pockets."

Chapter Sixteen
Peter and the Psychopomp

Davis didn't know what else to do but carry the small cage down the hall. He carefully kept the little white sheet over it from falling off. The cage might have been small, but what was inside was far from timid. Holding his breath, the middle-aged man pushed in the four-digit code by the locked door. Seconds later, it beeped, and the man entered.

He had told the office manager about the security breach, but he didn't feel like she seemed all too concerned. The man supposed it was because he had little to no memory of the events leading up to his clipboard's disappearance. He vaguely remembered Sally berating him for not getting Peter to cooperate and his idiotic idea involving the Psychopomp. He even remembered the splitting headache and a sweet voice telling him to relax, but that was all.

Betty had told the man that she could get his password changed on the first of the following week, and then she went on to tell him to keep an eye out for the clipboard. Davis figured the lady assumed he had too much on his mind and left it on a desk somewhere in the sister facility. Davis figured she could be right, and skated on hope he would walk into a room and find it sitting here untouched. It wasn't like Davis to lose chunks of time, and that bothered him as well, but not as much as the thought of Sally Wells discovering his monumental fuck up.

The thing in the cage chirped, and Davis looked down at it instinctively. It was a sweet sort of sound. The kind you would hear on a brisk spring morning while you were out for a stroll. As much as the man wanted to be comforted by the sound, he knew in his heart that the thing inside wanted to rip out his soul.

"You can give it up," Davis said calmly, surprising even him. "I know what you are, and I know if I let you out, you'll kill me and everyone in this Office." The chirping stopped, and seconds later, a hiss emerged from under the little sheet.

"I have no need for overindulgent souls." Is said. The words surfed on the tail of the hiss, wrapping themselves around the man's neck and tightening momentarily before wafting off down the hall.

Walking down the hall, through the door that had opened, Davis side-eyed each creature as he passed. They were all in their own rooms alone. Some of them were in straight jackets and others in hospital gowns, but one thing was the same in each... The 9-inch-thick bulletproof plexiglass that divided them from freedom. Lingering at the cell neighboring Peter's, the man stopped briefly, tightening the grip on the cage's handle. He didn't know if it was a stalling tactic or if he genuinely wanted to look in on the man sitting on the bed in the corner.

His head was down, and his long, greying hair was pulled back in a messy bun. He was tall and broad-shouldered, but he didn't have much muscle to speak of. There was a plate on the floor, and the food on it hadn't been touched. Steak and potatoes smothered in beef gravy. It was always the same with Rhudis. Even though the Rougarou was given restaurant worthy meals, he barely ate. When he finally did, it was only the vegetables. Lifting his hand, the man tapped on the glass, attempting to get the wolves' attention. Rhudis weakly lifted his head and snarled at Davis.

"Why don't you eat something? You look famished."

Wriggling his bare toes, Rhudis leaned forward on the bed where he sat and grinned just enough for Davis to see the man's pearly white teeth. His left K9 had been ripped from its socket.

"Why don't you come in here and give me something that will stick to my bones?" He asked. The low growl in his voice was bowel shaking, and even though he was on the other side of the glass that had been anointed with uncrossing oils and framed in Devil's shoestring, Davis quaked in his shoes as he looked upon the face of a coldblooded killer.

"You see," The hissing voice under the sheet began. "I'm nothing like him. I am only here to help you cross over. It would be peaceful, like falling asleep in your comfy recliner. The one you love in Office 12." Recoiling, Davis looked down at the birdcage in his hand, leaving Rhudis without so much as another word. How could Muhish know about the recliner? Did Psychopomps have the ability to read minds? No, that's not possible. The creature must have seen it while he was being transported. That's all it was… Or at least that's what Davis hoped.

Peter's cell had been redecorated, and the ancient sigils that adored the lining of the golden birdcage Davis was holding had been replicated perfectly. Unlike the other monsters in Office 6, Peter was still allowed to wear his dark suit. He still had his shoes and most of his dignity. During the scuffle, Lavita had punched the man in the face, leaving a rather nasty black eye. Still, it had begun to heal, leaving just a halo of purple and green accentuating his already deep, aging eyes. Smiling, Davis chewed on the corner of his lip for a moment before speaking.

"Lavita's got one hell of a right hook, doesn't she?" Shrugging, Peter crossed his arms and tapped his foot but stayed planted firmly in the middle of his cell.

"Where's Zanza?" Peter asked. That was always the first question he asked when he saw Davis. Even if Davis knew, he didn't think Peter would like the answer.

"I figure Sally put him with Sasha. That was what he wanted. Wasn't it? To be reunited with his niece?" Peter was unamused at the comment, and Davis could tell by the smug expression on the necromancer's face. "I want to do something for you. Something Sally would absolutely hate, but I've got to try. I'm giving you one last chance at helping us before this gets… Messy."

"What the hell is that supposed to mean?" Peter asked as he tapped his foot even harder on the floor beneath him. "You and your cohorts have already made this less than acclimatable when you threw us in your shoddy prison. I was more than willing to help you before all of this."

Davis knew Peter was telling the truth, but that ship had sailed. The second Kasey went flying through the grate during that damned meeting; Sally had been screaming inside job! While Davis agreed that someone on the inside had to have let the woman in, he highly doubted that it had been either Zanza or Peter. Of course, telling Sally they had a mole working for them was impossible. Whenever the subject was brought up, she would clap her hands and reply.

'All our staff are thoroughly vetted. There is no mole, just bad judgment in thinking we could trust the dead.' At the end of the day, Davis supposed it was easier for the woman to assume that a stranger could cross her than someone she knew. It helped her sleep at night, and for that, he couldn't fault her.

"I'm deeply sorry that my boss overreacted, and I've attempted to correct her mistake but I doubt there's anything else I can do at this juncture. Please, Mr. Nightingale, don't make me do what she's asking me to." Pushing himself closer to the glass, Davis looked down at the little opening near the floor. It had been made earlier in the day, and it was just big enough for the door to the birdcage to be pressed against it. Once Davis slid the door open, the Psychopomp would be sucked into the cell with Peter and almost impossible to reign back in. "All you have to do is bring him back. This could all be over with, and you'd have your humanity back. Why do you insist on making this difficult." Running his hand through his dark hair, Peter rolled his eyes and sighed.

"I've had time to think about it, and maybe feelings ARE overrated. Maybe I've decided against them... I mean, if I had them right now, I'd probably be hopping mad, right? That wouldn't bode well for you and your company because the only thing longer than our lifespans, Mr. Kellerman, is our grudges." Davis didn't like the sound of Peter's threats but he couldn't be persuaded to do anything other than what Sally had wanted. He knew that if he crossed her, he would be in the cell across from Rhudis and Peter, and then there wouldn't be anyone there who could keep Sally reeled in.

Kneeling down, Davis pushed the little golden cage against the opening along the floor of Peter's cell. Lifting the sheet, the man grabbed the latch to the lock on the cage's opening.

"It was nice knowing you, Mr. Nightingale. Hopefully, we can figure out a common ground... One where Muhish doesn't eat you alive."

Looking down at the cage, Peter stared at the white bird inside. It looked like any other dove he'd seen walking through the fields of Hashenshire, but that all began to change when Davis opened the cage door, and the feathered beast wasted no time flying inside.

"So you've chosen to give me a pet?" Peter asked smugly as the bird flew around the room, finally perching itself on Peter's shoulder.

"I'm hardly anyone's pet." The bird hissed. Standing back up, Davis studied Peter's face, waiting for a reaction to the bird's comment. If Peter was startled by it, the man showed no hint.

"I'll leave you two to it then," Davis exclaimed as he flung the sheet over his shoulder, sauntering off towards the doorway where he had come.

"Who are you?" Peter asked as he reached over and coaxed the bird onto his finger. It obliged a few moments later. "You're not just a talking bird. If that were the case, they wouldn't have bothered bringing you up here to me." The little white dove cooed, tilting its bobbing head to the left and then to the right.

"You may not recognize me, young man, but I certainly remember you." Opening its arms, the bird flew from the man's finger and then shifted and changed in midair. It was a grotesque display as the Psychopomp shifted from bird to snake to bear to deer and back again. Finally, it stopped on a figure Peter recognized immediately. Muhish was a man with dark skin, and black hair that was hidden mostly inside a turban. His golden robes hung across his body like a finely tailored suit, complementing his amber-shaded eyes. The Psychopomp looked unamused and more than a little irritated to be stuck inside a room with a parasite like Peter. He'd rather chew him up and spit him out than talk to him, but he learned long ago that he couldn't just act on any old impulse. His actions had consequences and this situation, the one that had gotten him into this jam in the first could finally be rectified if they could work together.

"You're death," Peter stated flatly. "Have you come to collect all the time I've stolen? Was that what you were supposed to do, I'm assuming, for your freedom?" This time, the Psychopomp smirked and shrugged his shoulders.

"I don't think that your human counterparts understand how I work. I do not need to eat; therefore, I do not need your souls. I merely take them and move them from one realm to the other. That does not mean I do not feel the urge to pick you up and wring you out like an old dish rag." Muhish took a few steps towards the man and stopped when he noticed Peter flinch. "I do not intend to hurt you... At least not until we are both out of this place. It's not fair to trap you like a rat... Where's the sportsmanship in that?"

It wasn't lost on Peter that the man standing before him could take all his power. There was nothing he could do, not with his own powers stripped. The kitchen staff in Office 6 were more than knowledgeable about what to feed each cryptid to keep them weak. For Peter, it was a constant flow of Khat and Lobelia. It slowed his ability to heal; therefore, all his magical properties went to retaining his health. He tried not to eat at all, and that worked for a few days until he passed out. When he woke up, he was hooked to an IV. Peter had no idea how long they had pumped him full of toxins. Then, he decided that eating just enough to stay alive was better because he could at least control how much was in his system.

"Fine. I call a parlay until we find ourselves on equal ground." Nodding at the Psychopomp, Peter relaxed a little and pointed at the bed. "You're welcome to sit if you like. We might be here for a while."

"Something tells me that might not be the case," Muhish replied. The man in the golden robes did not attempt to move from the spot where he was. There was something about his mannerisms that concerned Peter.

"Why do you say that?" Peter asked. He kept an eye on the Psychopomp but tried to look nonchalant about it.

"Now that we are in the room together, we have more than one option for escape. I've done the math in my head and decided that one in particular has the highest success rate. You may not like it, but as I said, it may be the best." Clapping his hands, Peter rubbed them together and smiled crookedly.

"Lay it on me."

"I can tell that you've noticed my nonmovement. Unfortunately, I've been deprived of the one thing that brings me power… The other realm. Every day that passes is a day that draws me nearer and nearer to immobility. Soon, I'd be nothing more than a statue, the wind by the sea, a mountain... I'd be nothing more than where I came from."

"Is that you're version of dying?" Peter asked. Muhish shook his head.

"Not exactly. You see, we can be brought back from stagnation. It's more of a punishment for not doing..." Looking up at the sky, Muhish lifted an eyebrow.

"Are we talking theology?" Peter began, but the reaper just laughed.

"Do we have to?"

"I prefer we didn't."

"Alright then." Straightening up, Muhish took a deep breath and continued. "I need a boost. Offer me one of your souls and access to your body... But before you do that, defile the sigils on the glass. Try not to make it too obvious so they won't see it coming."

"See what coming?" Peter asked.

"The next part of the plan."

Chapter Seventeen
Welcome to Hotel Oh Hell

"I can't believe you did that. No, wait, scratch that. Yes, I can. It's just like you to leave someone high and dry when they need you the most. Now we are down one person, and we didn't even get what we came for." Pacing the floor of the grimy hotel bedroom, Kasey placed her hands behind her back as she stared Neith down. The siren could tell that Kasey was beyond upset.

"Well, maybe if you weren't being such a baby about Muhish, you would have tagged along, and we could have gotten what we came for! You know, I only agreed to help you all if you got me close enough to the boy for me to escape with him. You weren't even in the same building!"

"I saw enough to know you fucked up!" Kasey said as she stopped in front of Neith. Clapping her hands together the woman came in close, almost touching noses with the girl. "You left her there for dead, and for all we know, that's what she is. Even if we could call Smita for help, how can I explain losing Birdie? Huh? How could I glaze over the fact that she's trapped in Office 6 with the others?"

The evening Neith had come to the apartment, it all made sense to the trio. Take the yellow truck, drive out to Office 6, steal the Psychopomp, and then release it on the Wendigo in Office 12. Neith and Kasey had even worked on a vessel to hold Muhish in. Of course, it only looked like a decorative shoebox with golden sigils to Beatrice, but the other two seemed quite pleased with themselves.

Kasey refused to be a part of the kidnapping. She offered to stay behind at the little hotel and do some remote work while Neith and Birdie took all the chances. It wasn't like Kasey not to get into the thick of it, but coming face to face with her ferryman didn't sound like a good time to her. Especially when she didn't know what kind of mood he was in. How long had they had him in chains? How long had he been holding a grudge for her escape from the veil? How hard was he going to come after her if he escaped? There were too many variables to take that kind of chance.

It had all started out wonderfully. The duo stood outside of the front door with protection bags around their necks. Neith used her powers of persuasion to get one of the doctors who had just started their shift to let them in. Kasey watched fervently through her crystal ball as they went to the basement. Surprisingly, the security was light once they entered, but the Psychopomp had already been moved when they had gotten to the cell... And all that was left in the basement was a talkative fairy named Quill.

Each basement was called Office 3. Some of them were color-coded, and some weren't. The only thing that the offices had in common was the inhabitants. Somewhere, someone had labeled each of them too volatile, too wild and unpredictable or strong to be used. The only thing Birdie and Neith could imagine Quill being was too damned talkative. His little pink arms smacked the glass as his eyes widened in excitement.

"Can you let me out? There's somewhere I've got to be. I'm not supposed to be here. My mom's gonna kill me." The lights in the basement began to flicker and brighten as the little fairy became more and more fidgety.

"I think we should get out of here." Neith had said, but before she knew what was going on, the guards had grabbed their arms, dragging them to the first available cell. Throwing them inside, they shut it and went to tell the others about who had been caught. Fortunately, the little breathing holes in the glass were just big enough for Neith's octopus body to wriggle through and before Bridie knew what was happening, her partner had flown up the steps and out of sight.

"It didn't make sense for me to stick around, Kacey. The longer I was in observation, the harder it would have been for me to hide who I really am. Now you have me, and we can go back together." Suddenly, there was a knock at the door. Neith jumped, then covered her mouth with her hands.

"Did they follow you!!" Kasey asked with anger. "I bet they followed you!"

"No!" Neith replied. She wanted to sound sure but couldn't quite shake the quiver in her voice. "I used my glamour. They... they couldn't have."

Inching towards the door, Kasey pressed her eye against the peephole and then sighed. Seconds later, the door was open, and she was facing Smita, Raphiel, and Delilah.

"How did you find us?" Kasey asked.

"How couldn't we?" Delilah said with an eye roll. "You two parked that yellow monster right in the front." Jerking her head back, Kasey eyeballed Neith, whose cheeks became increasingly brighter.

"Sorry." It didn't take long for the Siren's eyes to drift toward the girl who had called her out. Neith wrinkled her nose as she put her hands on her hips cautiously. "Who are you?" She asked. Smita could tell it was a genuine question, but she could also sense an air of irritation in Neith's voice. The girl didn't like newcomers, especially ones that pointed out her mistakes.

"That's Delilah. She's the wolf that bit Raph... Or should I keep calling you Tom?" Shaking his head, the man shoved his hands into his pockets, unsure of how to answer the question.

"And you're just riding around with her? If I were you, I wouldn't trust one of those Rougarous that have tasted blood. I heard it's hard for them to kick the habit." Smita listened to Neith's quick retort and shrugged her shoulders.

"Well, if you let us in, We could explain it all in detail." Suddenly Smita stopped speaking, counting the people in the room and coming up one short. "Wait, where's Birdie? Didn't she come along with you two?" Stepping between Neith and Smita, Kasey ushered the trio inside, shutting the door behind them.

"I guess," Kasey began with exhaustion, "After you tell us what you've been up to, we've got a little explaining to do ourselves."

"So, where are you from? I don't really remember a lot about where I'm from... Except that, my mom's been waiting for me to come back, and I haven't seen her in a long time." I listened to the little boy speak from the other cell. It was hard to keep up with all the things he was saying. Sometimes, he would stop talking altogether, and I would think for a moment that he had tired himself out or vanished completely from his prison, but then he would pick up right where he left off with more excitement than before.

"I'm from Moondust Island," I replied absentmindedly.

"Oh wow... That sounds like a pretty place. I don't think that I've ever been. Does it have big trees and purple fruit?" Thinking about the question, I didn't really know how to respond.

How long had I been trapped down here anyway? It felt like forever. Since my capture, no one had bothered to come down to check on me. Not even Sally. I figured they didn't see the rush. I wasn't going anywhere anytime soon... Or so it seemed.

"Do you know what time it is?" I finally asked, choosing to ignore the previous question the boy had asked.

"Geez, lady, I don't really know. I feel sort of hyper, which means the moon is probably out. Did you know I'm one of the only breeds of Whimsy that can see in the dark? My mom used to say that's what made me special... That and my multicolored hair. I no longer have that; it's all turned yellow like the sun." I couldn't see the little pink motormouth in the cell beside mine, but in my mind, he had grabbed a handful of his own hair and was looking at it with his giant marble eyeballs. "There was this big war where I come from, and I managed to help everyone. I was scared the whole time I did, but I didn't let that stop me. Now, I'm not scared of anything. When the door to the other side opened, part of me slipped through. So now, I'm not really here, and I'm not really there... I'm not really anywhere, and I'm everywhere all at once! Isn't that funny?" Rolling my eyes, I leaned my head against the stone wall behind me. I had decided to sit on the floor against the towering mound of rubble that separated me from Quill. The whole day had passed, and Neith hadn't returned with Kasey. Part of me figured it was because the Vampire couldn't travel well while the sun was out, but another part of me feared that Neith had hightailed it out of there, leaving me to rot. I tried my best not to let the intrusive thoughts win. Shaking my head, I turned my attention to the boy in the cell beside mine.

"What do you mean? You're not everywhere; you're in a prison. Aren't you scared of that, at least?" There was a giggle from the emptiness of the hall. It sounded like how happy felt, and a bit of warmth trickled through my veins like a shot of honey fresh from the hive.

"I'm not in a prison," Quill said shortly. "Nothing on this plain can hold me for long. I'm merely here to pick something up, and then I'll be on my way." Snorting, I rolled my eyes again. I could understand why Quill would want to make believe he was a big hero. If I had been locked down in a dingy hole like this at his age, I would have peed my pants a long time ago.

"What is it you came to collect?" I asked the boy, entertaining his delusion.

"It's a weapon. Hope told me all about it before she left. She went on a long sleep. An explosion was followed by a great fire that burned down the Nematon. I'm not sure how to get back." There was a long pause, so I decided to poke a little further. I didn't see the danger because I was trapped down there just like him.

"Was Hope your mother?" I asked. There was another pause, and still, Quill didn't bother to answer.

"Did you know that our hair color tells everyone around us what we're good at? I think that's why my hair couldn't decide on a color until the war. I had a little bit of it all inside me. I was sampling from everyone in the town, holding in their talents until I really needed them... Sometimes I think I can see into the future a bit, you know? Not on purpose. I can't help it. I knew those people were coming through the portal to the great tree that night... I knew what was going to happen if we helped them..." I listened to the fairy speak even though I had no idea what he was babbling about. Something on the other side of the wall began to jingle. It sounded like the tinkering of bells, but I knew that couldn't be right.

"Who were the people you were helping? Were they bad people?" Suddenly, Quill appeared on the other side of the glass. His broad smile and angelic face brought joy to my heart. "How the hell did you get out of there?" I exclaimed as I jumped to my feet.

"I think I know why I've been down here waiting all this time. You see, I've been waiting for you."

"I don't follow." I continued.

"You have the same hair color as my best friend Flook. Raven black."

"What does that mean?" I asked as I pressed the palm of my hand against the glass.

"You're a great warrior, a wanderer. You're here to lead me to what I've been seeking."

"Kid, I'd love to." I began, "But I doubt I can do whatever it was you did to get out. I'm not a fairy." The smile fell from Quill's face as he put a finger in the air.

"First of all, I'm not a fairy. Fairies are nasty little monsters that explode when you pop them. I am a Mesmer, and I can help you. Can't you see my hair is golden yellow? It appears that's all I need to succeed in this realm."

"Yellow hair?" I asked. The wheels in my head were turning, but I still couldn't make a spark. Touching his finger to the glass, I heard the tinkling of bells again.

"No, magic, silly." Suddenly, the Plexiglas began to ebb and bend until it poofed into a cloud of orange smoke. Quill had managed to free me from my cage without breaking a sweat. Cautiously, I walked through the opening, looking at the boy in dismay.

"You could have done that all this time?" I couldn't believe what I was seeing. Maybe I had misjudged the kid from the start. Smita would have been disappointed. It was one of the first things she had tried to teach me.

'Never underestimate the opponent in front of you. Some of the most innocent-looking creatures are the most dangerous.'

"I didn't see a need to let us out until I had all my thoughts in order. If you help me find the weapon I'm looking for, I'll owe you a favor. Hey! You could even come to Whimsies Whispers with me. We always need warriors, especially after the Mare Moss incident at the great feast..." Quill's voice trailed off for a second as his eyes glazed over. I was starting to understand what he meant by not quite here or there. With a quivering hand, I reached out and touched the boy on the shoulder, but my fingers went right through him.

"Holy shit," I whispered. "You're an astral projection."

Chapter Eighteen
Neither Here nor There

It was all a blur. Everything that had happened and everything that was going to happen. Davis tossed and turned in his bed, wondering if he was going to be the bearer of bad news in the morning when he walked into the Office just to discover that Muhish had killed Peter. Or even worse, he'd walk in on Sally discovering it all in real-time. He wondered if he would scrape out of it with his life... And what the HELL had he done with that frigging clipboard? Closing his eyes only brought visions of what might be. Nothing in his life was predictable anymore, and that was torture for a man set in his ways.

Rolling over in bed, Davis looked at the clock on his bedside stand and groaned. Only two more hours to go, and then he would have to face the music one way or another.

"I might as well get up." He mumbled to himself as he sat up. Running a hand through his tousled hair, Davis put his bare feet on the floor, allowing his toes to sink into the thicket of carpet he had just gotten installed. The drapes framing the window by the bathroom door hung open carelessly as the waning moon tickled the frame with blushing light from above. Soon, he thought, the sun would be rising, and so would Sally's temper. His mind went to the what-if section in a fleeting moment. What if he just got in his car, drained his accounts, and moved to another country? How long could he make it before Sally and Lavita caught up with him? The idea was a fun one for about five seconds. He knew better than to cross the company. Even running away from them was an act of treason in Sally's eyes. Once you were in, you were in all the way. Davis wasn't going to get out without a hell of a fight... Or in a body bag.

Making his way to the kitchen, the man looked down at his pajamas. They reminded him of a prison jumpsuit. They were full cotton and comfortable but about a size too big and adorned with large white and blue vertical stripes. Davis wasn't sure what had impulsed him to buy the sleepwear. Maybe in the back of his mind, he knew he was in his own version of prison. It didn't look like it to the outside world, but Mr. Kellerman was just as much a slave to

Lupin Corp as the monsters in the Offices he visited. He could do nothing more than make some fancy coffee and face the music.

Davis had just started making his breakfast when there was a knock at the door. It was soft at first. So soft, in fact, that he thought maybe the neighbors had shut their car doors too loudly. The second time the knock came, it was a little louder, more hurried, and upsetting. Lowering his eyebrow, Davis opened the kitchen drawer and pulled out a knife. There was no way anyone pleasant would be on the other side of that knock. It was still far too early for anyone in Office 6 to have discovered Peter, and that only left one other option.

As Davis exited the kitchen, he padded across the living room floor, holding the knife up and away from his face, ready to strike anyone on the other side.

"Who's there!" Davis yelled as he drew closer to the door. No one said a word, but in response, the knock continued. This time it was so hard, the man could see the wood straining against the pressure. A small crack had begun to form in the middle, around five or so feet from the floor. Davis wanted to walk closer, but his feet refused. Stopping in the middle of the living room, the man stared blankly at the blue door.

Suddenly, there was another knock. This time, it only came once because once was all that was needed for Davis's front door to come flying off its hinges. The man barely had time to jump out of the way as the door flew across the room, stopping only when it had contacted the far wall. Falling onto the couch, Davis lost his grip as the knife fell softly to the floor.

"What the hell!" The man screamed. It was more of a reaction than a question. He knew what the hell... He'd been waiting for it for some time now. That's what playing with fire will get you.

Stomping through the door, Smita looked over at the man with a bitter expression. She didn't hesitate. She didn't even bat an eye. Kicking the knife out of the way, she lumbered over to Davis Kellerman and snatched him up by the collar. Seconds later, the man was standing in front of her, not by choice, but because she was holding him there. His feet didn't actually touch the ground. If he stretched his toes, he thought he could feel the tickle of carpet... But then again, that might have been wishful thinking.

"I believe you have a friend of mine. I would like her back now. Oh, and I plan on breaking a finger for every hair you've knocked out of place."

"How are you so strong?" Davis choked as he put both hands in the air. Throwing the man back down on the couch, Smita ignored the question. She hovered over him like a vulture staring down roadkill. She was bloodthirsty. Davis's eyes widened as he watched her eyes with fascination. They flickered honeypot brown, and then gold, and then back to brown again.

"I didn't know you felt so strongly about Peter," Davis exclaimed as he scooted back into his seat. He began to tremble a little, which only enraged Smita more.

"Don't play stupid with me, Davis! I know you have Birdie, and I want her back."

"Birdie? That little bookworm of yours? What would we want with her?" Grabbing the man by the collar again, Smita closed her fist, ready to hit him, but then she stopped. Her eyes locked onto his, and her expression changed completely.

"You... You really don't know, do you?" She asked.

"What? What don't I know?" Davis stammered. His hands were still up around his face. He was terrified of Smita; that much was for certain.

"No one contacted you about the breach?" Smita asked. "I was told… By a friend that they have Birdie in a cell in the basement of Office 6. They call it Office 3, right?" Suddenly, a loud and uncomfortable laugh rattled its way out of Davis's throat.

"No one put your friend in Office 3. No one with a brain would go down there. If she managed to get into Office 6, which I doubt, AND make it to the bottom, there wouldn't be anyone there to greet her. Muhish was the only one in that dingy hole and I gave him an upgrade before I left yesterday."

"That can't be," Smita exclaimed as she lightened her grip on the 100% Cotton pajama top. "She told me two guards pushed them into the cell beside that little fairy guy. He was talking too much, and the guards overheard. You're lying to me."

"Why would I lie to you," Davis said. The quiver in his voice had begun to leave as the anger in Smita's eyes vanished. "If someone had breached the gate, I would have been notified. If someone had been captured, they wouldn't have put them in the hole, and the most important thing about your story is if someone were to scream in Office 3, no one would have heard it. There were no guards. That whole basement is soundproof. We call the basements Office 3 for a reason. Those rooms are soundproof, bulletproof, and waterproof. We do all our best work down there." Smita didn't want an elaboration on what 'our best work' meant. Instead, she backed away and allowed Davis to get up. Putting her hands on her forehead, the woman began to pace a bit, but she didn't take her eyes off the man standing in front of her. Laughing a little to herself, she groaned and then stopped.

"I did exactly what I told Kasey not to do. I came in here half-cocked, thinking I could intimidate you into helping me." Falling to her knees, Smita let her hands fall to her sides. To Davis, she looked deflated, defeated, and hopeless. If he had really wanted to, he thought he might have been able to run out of the door and make it to his car, but something inside of him didn't want to anymore. He'd been in a similar position, and he thought maybe things wouldn't have gotten so out of control if he had had someone in his corner.

Kneeling, Davis grabbed one of Smita's hands and gave it a squeeze. She wasn't expecting it and almost recoiled at the touch.

"I'm tired," Davis said with a sigh. "I'm tired of all of this. My feud with Kasey has gotten boring, and now... With what Sally's trying to do... I, no, WE have to put a stop to it."

"Are you offering your services?" Smita asked, a little flabbergasted. Davis thought about the question and nodded.

"Yes, I think I am, but once this is over, you've got to get me off this island. It won't be safe for any of us. She'll retaliate; that much is a fact." Holding her breath, Smita nodded slowly as they both got to their feet.

"What's she trying to do?" Smita asked. "Who's this guy everyone's so afraid of?" Far off in the distance, Davis could hear the first songbirds of the morning. It wouldn't be long now before the sun would come up, and the discovery of what he had done would be brought to light.

It wasn't an accident. He wanted the Psychopomp to kill Peter. It wasn't anything personal. Davis just couldn't risk letting Thomas Henderson walk with the living again.

"There's so much your friends don't know. Tell them to come in, and I'll explain everything."

Chapter Nineteen
Death Takes Many Forms

Promptly at 8:30 AM, Sally walked through the front doors of Office 6. The lady at the front desk stood aloof and disinterested in the older lady's arrival. Staring down at her phone, the receptionist popped her gum and waved the lady through without so much as a word. Lavita wasn't too far behind, sniffing the air as she followed her mother through the metal detector. Stopping in the lobby, Sally bobbed her thumb over to the new girl behind the desk.

"Who is that?' She asked the guard who was stationed at the stairwell. Shrugging, the man in the brown uniform looked down at his clipboard and huffed.

"She's a temp from Office 1. Looks like our regular, Tracy Lannirday, had a family emergency." Lowering his brow, he snorted a little and shook his head. "That can't be right."

"What?" Sally asked, attempting to look over the man's shoulder.

"It says here she has to attend a funeral."

"What's so weird about that?" Sally retorted. Snatching the clipboard, Sally looked at the paper and then snorted. "For her housecat's cousin's brother-in-law?"

"I... I don't know." The guard stuttered. "I'll look into it."

"You better." Sally hissed as she handed the board back to the man. Lavita snorted in agreeance as the duo pushed past the guard and up the steps to the second floor. "I can't believe this, Lavita. Doesn't anyone know what day it is? I have a good feeling that today will be the day Peter finally comes around to our way of thinking." Lavita snorted again, only this time it was a longer more drawn-out sound. Stopping id-stride, Sally turned around and pushed a finger into her daughter's chest for a moment. Sally's wrinkled face was contorted into a grimace.

"Don't you start doubting me too!" Sally exclaimed. "Of course, putting Muhish in the same room as the necromancer was a good idea. We don't know much about either of them, but they had to be natural enemies... It just makes sense." Grunting again, Lavita lifted an eyebrow. This caused Sally to go off the rails even more.

"What do you MEAN Peter might be dead? There's no way! That man thrives on death! Muhish is literally the definition of that! If anyone is gone, it's going to be Muhish."

Looking up from her phone, the girl behind the counter grinned slightly. She had an earbud in one ear and a speaker attached to the collar of her work shirt.

"Man, she sure is wound up tight... Speaking of wound up, are you okay... Not that I care, but man, you downed a LOT of energy drinks before you kicked in that dude's door." Staring back at her on the phone's screen was Smita. The girl behind the counter couldn't quite make out where the woman was, but that didn't matter much to her.

"I'm fine, Delilah... Just make sure you get out of there when I tell you to and not a second earlier. This is a phishing expedition, info only. You remember the code?" nodding, Delilah gave the woman on the other line a thumbs up.

"Who would have guessed that a slimy Octopus lady would have come in so handy." There was a huff from the staircase as the two women began their ascent to the second floor, vanishing from Delilah's sight.

Rounding the corner, Sally saw yet another new face. This one was at the door to Office 6, fumbling with the control panel. He would push in a few buttons and then an error message would appear. He looked frustrated.

"Can I help you?" Sally asked with irritation. "This is a secure facility. No one can come in without proper authority." Turning around, the man in the white lab coat stared down at the old lady with a stern face.

"I'm assuming no one told you I was coming from Office 1?" he asked confusedly. "That's a real tight ship you've got running here, Ms. Wells." The man was tall and thin. He wore a pair of thick glasses that accentuated his already larger-than-normal hazel eyes. His dark hair was pulled back in a messy man-bun, and his thin lips were perched just above a clean-shaven and predominant chin.

"You seem to know who I am, but by your attitude, you may not know my position. I sign your checks, Mr…" Leaning in, the woman eyeballed the tall man's plastic badge. "Mr. Weiner?" The man tried not to laugh, but it was almost impossible.

"It's pronounced, Winner. It's French. Just call me Tom. These temporary codes don't seem to be working today. It might have something to do with the new receptionist you have downstairs. We've had problems with her in 1 as well."

Something about Tom's knowledge of the new girl brought Sally a little ease. Nodding, she brushed past him and typed in her code, then pressed her finger against the pad beside it.

"As soon as Mr. Kellerman arrives, we'll get started."

"About that." Tom began with a sigh. "Davis is going to be late today… A family emergency, I believe."

"Is that so?" Sally replied. The doors to Office 6 whooshed open, and the trio walked through without any more disruption. "What was his excuse?"

"His goldfish has the flu. You know pets are like family to some people." Tom retorted quickly.

"The… Flu? How would you know if your fish had the flu?" Shrugging, Tom followed the two women down the hall.

"I would suspect the bubbles would be all snotty." Lavita made an odd guttural sound, and Sally snorted in response. Tom tried to keep his head down, but it was hard seeing all the others trapped behind the glass. Some looked content to sit alone, others paced, and still others screamed and hollered, tied up in straight jackets. Approaching the last of the cells, Sally all but ignored Rhudis. Tom, on the other hand, couldn't. The tall man was sitting as still as a statue in the middle of his bunk, his feet tucked comfortably under him. Someone had let him out of his straight jacket, or so it seemed. It sat folded in the middle of the floor beside a plate of rotting food.

'Did she finally come for me?' a heavy voice asked inside Tom's head. It took him by surprise, and he stumbled back, covering one ear with his free hand.

"Not so loud, dude!"

"Excuse me?" Sally asked as he attention turned from Peter's cell to the man beside her.

"Sorry," Tom exclaimed with an absent laugh. He pretended to pull something out of his ear and shoved the imaginary thing into his pants pocket. "I forgot I still had my headset on." Rolling her eyes, Sally turned back to the man of the hour. "Dude, you're making me look like a loon!" Tom whispered as he lifted his eyebrows. Lavita turned her head back to the man in the white lab coat for a second but quickly lost interest. He figured she knew she could take him if it came down to it.

'That's not my intent. I could smell you both the moment you walked in the door. You've come to liberate me, haven't you.'

"Among other things," Tom whispered. Finally, the man on the bunk looked up at Tom. He had piercing grey eyes and one of the strongest jawlines Tom had ever seen.

'Why don't you speak to me internally? Don't you know how?' This time, Tom didn't answer; he just shook his head. Gritting his teeth, the Rougarou closed his eyes in irritation. *'Of course, you're new. Probably an accident Delilah made because I haven't been around to teach her. There's so much more to us, Raphiel. So much more than just the wolf. You can control it. It doesn't control you.'*

Pressing her hand against the glass, Sally watched Peter as he stood in the middle of the cell. He looked exactly the same as he had the day before. She wondered if Davis had forgotten to put the Psychopomp in with him before he clocked out.

"Peter?" Sally asked as she looked the Necromancer in the eye. "Are you alright?" Twitching a bit, Peter attempted a smile, which looked much more like a grimace.

"I'm fine. It took more out of me than I would care to admit, but I fear I've outmatched your reaper. This place had grown a bit... Stale and I've decided to help you as long as you release Zanza and Sasha."

"I believe that can be arranged," Sally replied as she relaxed a little. "I'll grant you three safe passage home. Only after you do what I ask."

"Of course," Peter muttered. Lacing his fingers together, the man patiently waited for Sally to open the door. Everything was going to plan until Raphiel fell back against the wall, holding his head with his hands.

"Mr. Weiner, what on earth has gotten into you?!" Sally exclaimed, but all Raphiel could do was groan in pain. Ripping his glasses off, the man rubbed his eyes. When he pulled back his palms, all he could see was red.

'I'm trying to teach you. I'm trying to show you. Why are you fighting me?'

Rushing to the man's aid, Lavita scooped him up and rushed him to the closest unoccupied room. It happened to be the office of Ulrich Tandy, one of the lower-level shareholders. Lying him on the couch, Lavita knelt down on one knee, brushing the blood from his cheeks. The pain had started out unbearable, but as the images began to grow clearer, Raphiel's pain began to subside.

"Thank you, Lavita," Raphiel whispered. "Please, tell your mother I'll be along to help as soon as I can. I just need a minute or two."

Nodding, the large woman walked out of the room, shutting the door behind her.

'You aren't even linked to us. Not fully, anyway. That's why I cannot show you all the things I want to. Why haven't you fed? You're not at full strength.'

"Dude. You don't get it. I don't want to be part of your club. I want out. I'm here to get you and hopefully break this damned curse." There was a long pause before Rhudis replied.

'Who do you think we are, Raphiel? We aren't Werewolves. There's no indoctrination. Either you are or you aren't. Though the waxing and waning moon increase our cycles, we ultimately control who we are... And what we eat. The hunger inside you will eventually win. You must satiate it soon, or you'll turn on your friends.'

"I... I don't believe you. Delilah she only turns on the full moon. She changes and feeds. She turns into a wolf. I've seen it. She told me you do, too. That you only eat meat once a month, during the full moon. You bit Kasey, and you were a wolf. I've already killed my two best friends."

'We do what we think is most natural. In Western culture, it's the wolf, but if we were raised elsewhere, we might become eagles in flight, sea creatures, or even cave-dwelling insects. We can trans-mutate into whatever our collective conscious wants us to. As I've *said before, we're pulled by the cycle of the moon but not a slave to it like our Lycanthropic counterparts. As for your friends, unless they were chickens, you had no part in their deaths.'*

Sitting up on the couch, Raphiel wiped the blood from his eyes as he finally caught his bearings.

"Well then, if I didn't do it and Delilah didn't do it, then who the hell did."

'My guess would be the Corporation. I've kept my ear to the ground and know a thing or two about the man in the blue bulb. They plan on moving Peter over there today... And it isn't good. There was talk about collecting a few parts for his reconstruction. I'm assuming they took the parts they needed and then mauled the bodies, so it looked like an attack.' Scrambling to his feet, Raphiel ran to the door and opened it with some force. *'What are you doing?'* Rhudis asked.

"I've got to tell the others! There's no time."

"Mr. Weiner, are you feeling better? what on earth are you on about now?" Sally asked as she jerked her body towards the open door.

"I... Uh, I forgot to turn off the hotplate in my room. The whole place could go up. Catch you on the flip!"

Chapter Twenty
The Story of Thomas the Terror

In the early 1990s, Nanjoglobe decided to start an experiment known only as 'The Thomas Project.' Headed by well-known environmentalist and microbiologist Penelope Hillsdale, the project, in its infancy, was an astounding success. During the course of Thomas's very young life, he had already defeated stillbirth by the reanimation of dead tissue. He exceeded their expectations and jumped every milestone with exuberance and undying enthusiasm.

Penelope thought it was all going to plan until phase three was initiated. Thomas was given a round of shots at every meal and then exposed to every element one could think of. Sometimes, it was disease; other times, drowning, fire, asphyxiation, and psychological torture. Seeing such a small child treated in that way broke the woman's heart. It took a horribly taxing toll on her.

Hillsdale hadn't realized how close she had grown to the little boy until it all came to a head. Thomas had hit a roadblock in his evolution. Not only had he become defiant in his orders to obey when they brought him in for his 'treatments,' but he had also become increasingly unpredictable. Some days, he would be sweet and caring, and others, he would attempt to kill whoever was around him. Eventually, around his fourth birthday, Penelope was given the orders to terminate the experiment. All she had to do was kill the poor boy. It wasn't like he hadn't been through it a million times before. Without jolting him back to life, Thomas would die a natural death and rot away in a coffin like everyone else in the known world.

Eventually, Penelope succumbed to the request and took the boy away from the facility for the last time. Driving him across town to a local bakery, the two of them ate their fill of cupcakes and pastries before going back to a little house Hillsdale had acquired at the beginning of the experiment.

100 Bluecrest Ave wasn't just a little home away from home. It had a hidden room behind a bookcase with soundproof walls in the back. Leading the boy to his death, Penelope tried her

best to keep a cool head. She struggled with the repercussions of killing such an innocent child. He wasn't asked to be brought into this world, and she had forced him anyway. Playing evolution was one thing, but finally, she realized she couldn't play God. Fishing around in her pocketbook, Hillsdale pulled out a syringe, filled to the 8mm mark with a bright blue substance. Calmly, she explained to the boy that it was just another injection like all the others and that if he took it, he wouldn't have to take it anymore, ever again. Of course, Thomas aptly agreed. It didn't take long, thirty or forty minutes, and the poor kid was lying dead on the floor of her little makeshift lab. It wasn't what she wanted, but it was what had happened. The new M1 concoction apparently still had too many kinks in it to fully work.

As they say, you can take the scientist out of the lab, but you can't take the lab out of the scientist. While Penelope had no intentions of bringing the boy back, she felt compelled to find out what had stopped the boy's heart. After all, M1 was supposed to fix what ailed you, not help it along. That's when she discovered all the abandoned pathways in the boy's brain. It explained his violent outbursts and why he acted so differently all the time. Each time the kid died, his brain reacted differently. Essentially, he was a new person. Sometimes, he would retain his memories; other times, he wouldn't. Of course, if left alone long enough, his memories would eventually return. The brain is odd like that. Still, she was no closer to the cause of his death than when she had started.

One night in early September of 2000, Penelope had fallen asleep in her little laboratory. It had been a little over a week since the injection that had killed Thomas, and the woman had taken blood samples, brain samples, and even bone samples of the boy. Tonight though, it wasn't bad dreams that had awakened her.

On the table, under the sheet where the boy's boy laid, wrapped in a cooling bag, she could see movement. It was slight at first, but then, it grew more obvious. Rushing to Thomas's side, she opened the bag to be met with a set of giant, crying blue eyes. All the open wounds she had left on him were healed. Only red marks were left, like memories of a past life.

Penelope knew that she couldn't keep Thomas. She had already told Nanjoglobe that the boy was deceased, and they had pulled the plug on the whole thing... But she wasn't going to kill him, not again. After taking a few more samples of blood, Hillsdale whisked the boy away to a private adoption center... One that wouldn't ask too many questions. Eventually, in 2004, Thomas was adopted by Quinn and Linus Henderson. They knew the boy was special but didn't know just how special.

Over the course of his lifetime, Thomas would die and come back multiple times. Each story is more unbelievable than the next; only one undeniable fact held them all together... Thomas was unkillable.

Nanjoglobe was the mother company that had started it all. What once started as a small medical company quickly became a conglomerate with its fingers in everyone's pies. Marcus Goodhope had found a collection of epithelial cells in the Arizona desert. His original visit was one of leisure, running away to have a tryst with his new girlfriend, Clarissa. No one knew where they had come from, but one thing was certain: they held a mystery that Marcus wanted to harness. The cells regenerated no matter how hard he tried to destroy them. They always came back stronger. Experiments A through L failed miserably, killing the host within days of injection. Marcus couldn't figure out where he was going wrong. Every subject was tested for illness and given a clean bill of health before going into the trials... And then someone suggested using a cadaver. That's where Thomas took the stage. Nanjoglobe thought they had turned over every stone and looked at every variable before ultimately deciding to terminate The Thomas Project, but that wasn't quite true. Once Thomas was injected with that pure strain of M1, the skin cells that had ultimately given him life began to mutate... Learning from the predators that had taken his life over and over again, they began to use fire, ice, disease, and mind control to alter the people around him and create a safer environment for the host to thrive. It wouldn't have been fair to call Thomas a real boy because even from conception, he was simply a host for something greater... A walking, talking, God Particle.

"I want cake! Not like a single piece, but the whole cake. I want chocolate! No, strawberry! Yes! With double frosting and a candle. You know, I think Mom forgot my birthday last year. I don't remember having a cake with candles." I stood there listening to Quill ramble on, unsure how to stop him. Every time I opened my mouth to interrupt, the little man would glitch. Sometimes, his marble eyes would glaze over, and other times, he would literally turn into television static and then disappear for a few minutes, only to return and start rambling all over.

The first time Quill vanished, I made my way down the dark hallway and back up to the steps, only to be met with a locked door. It didn't look like the door I had gone down earlier; it looked like it hadn't been opened in ages. The lock was rusty, and the handle was old and haggard with dents and cuts along its grip. The longer I spent down there, the more I noticed things around me beginning to change. I hadn't paid it any mind at first, seeing as I was new to the environment and guessed I had just missed some of the prison's nuances. Now, though, I was all but convinced Quill was manipulating the basement. The concrete floor had quickly changed to cobblestone, and the glass that separated all the cells had vanished, and in its place were old rotten bars. One by one, firelit torches began to adorn the walls as Quill continued to speak.

"I love cake, but not as much as pie! Cherry pie, peach pie... Oh! You can't forget the gooseberries." My mind was going a mile a minute. I had to find a way to get through to the little Mesmer. I tried to think back to the section in the book about Astral Projection. It was one of the first things I had read. Maybe, I thought, the reason Quill was manipulating his surroundings was because he was becoming more self-aware. Maybe he's recreating a place from the home he longs to return to. It hadn't dawned on me until now that the guards that had thrown Neith and myself into the cell beside Quill were dressed oddly. They hadn't looked like I would have expected. Were the guards really members of Lupin Corp, or were they projections of Quill's mind... And if they were the ladder, how strong was the boy really?

Getting down on one knee, I attempted to make eye contact with the Mesmer as he went on and on about cookies and gumdrops. His little eyes were positively glowing with happiness from the memories of his youth. I could tell that he spent a lot of time there, in his happy place. When he leaves, he loses his connection to himself. So, maybe he needed an anchor. Something that would give him hope.

"Quill. Do you want to play a game?" I asked with mock enthusiasm. Suddenly, the boy stopped talking. His smile was a mile wide as he shook his head with glee.

"Oh! I haven't played a game in a long time. What shall we play?" Looking up at the ceiling, I grinned a little.

"What about hide and seek?" Clapping his hands together, Quill jumped up and down. His image flashed a few times, and there, for a second, I thought I was going to lose him.

"I love hide and seek! Flook is the best at finding me." Suddenly, his excitement turned to concern as he looked around at the dingy floor around them. "There aren't a lot of places to hide around here. We're going to need more room."

"I couldn't agree more," I said as I tried to laugh, matching his energy as best as I could. "Do you think you could do the same thing to the door over there that you did to the prison glass?" I asked. "We could go up there and hide. I bet there are lots of cool spaces we haven't explored." Quill thought about it for a moment and then frowned.

"I suppose I could do that, but the last time I didn't do what I was told, things got extra icky. I don't want that to happen again."

"What do you mean?" I asked. I wasn't sure if this was going to be a rerun of what happened before. Whenever I tried to ask about the weapon he had spoken of earlier, his little body would glitch out. I didn't know if it was a defense mechanism or if he truly didn't want to tell me. Quill was all over the place emotionally, and for me, it felt a little like playing with a wet stick of dynamite.

"Well then, what if I gave you permission to leave? Has anyone said that to you before?" Again, Quill thought about my question and then smiled brightly.

"Well, you are an adult. I guess you would know best." Suddenly, a smell emerged from the cell beside me. I couldn't quite place it, but something told me it wasn't good. The rancid stench filled my nostrils and made me feel ill. Glancing through the bars, I began to notice an orange furry fungus growing from a crack near the ceiling.

"What the hell is that?" I asked, more to myself than to the little Mesmer in front of me. For the first time since I met the little boy, he gave me a straight answer.

"Oh, that's Mare Moss. Don't breathe that stuff in for too long, or you'll be a mindless shell of your old self." Suddenly, the floor beneath me began to quake, and the cobblestone crumbled a bit. The torches that lined the wall began to shake, casting long shadows in the hallway. "Come on!" Quill exclaimed as he ran to the stairs at the end of the hall. "Well, go up and play with the others."

"What do you mean?" I asked as I followed the young boy to the door. Brushing past Quill, I reached for the handle. Pushing the door open, I heard the screams of people on the other side.

Chapter Twenty-One
Welcome to Chaos Mountain

"Okay!" Quill said with excitement. "I'll hide first! You count to one hundred." Looking over my shoulder, the little Mesmer vanished. I hadn't the foggiest if he actually went and hid or if he had gone back down to the basement to continue his rant. At this point, it didn't really matter.

The first-floor lobby was a chaotic mess. Guards and visitors screamed as they ran from the monsters that once were trapped behind glass. I didn't know how long I could stay hidden. One thing was for sure: I didn't want to go back down to Office 3. I had a sure exit, and I wasn't going to lose it. Suddenly, something from behind the door I was holding grunted, and the metal shield was ripped from my embrace. I trembled as I looked into the face of Holly Grove.

"Lavita," I whispered. Without responding, the giant woman took one beefy hand and snatched me up by the back of my neck. I struggled, trying with all my might to get her to release me, but it was no use. She was far too strong. "Let me go!" I insisted, but Lavida didn't answer to me. Someone from another floor must have pulled an alarm because seconds later, a loud horn began to blare, followed by a canned voice that began instructing the patrons inside to leave the building in a single field line. My shirt was tugged tight against my throat, making it hard to breathe. I knew that if she didn't let go soon, I would lose consciousness completely. I kicked my feet and pulled back on my shirt with everything I had. I could hear the fibers around the collar beginning to rip.

I wasn't sure what it was that made the giant mutant stop in her tracks, but whatever it was matched her growl. It matched her malice, and I didn't know whether to be frightened or relieved.

'Let her go." The heavy voice commanded, but Lavita stomped her foot. My head felt swimmy, but even in my half-awake state, I knew how insane this was. There were monsters all around, and yet they chose to avoid the confrontation that had stopped between the stairwell to the second floor and the front desk. I was facing the doorway, resting my head on the back of Lavita's calf. She still had a death grip on my collar. The disinterested receptionist had been scooped up and whisked away by a tall man with bare feet. It was odd; I wasn't sure if I was hallucinating or not, but the man who vanished through the front door with the woman in his arms could have been Raphiel's older brother. His salt and pepper hair was pulled back in a messy bun, and his features favored my friend's.

"I said let her go NOW!" Those words brought me back to reality, just in time to see a wisp of light dance by, cutting a guard who had been on his walkie in half with ease. Blood spurted across the white linoleum floor, hitting the side of my face. Hot gore covered the lenses of my glasses, making it even harder for me to see what was going on. After that display, I was convinced it was more of a blessing than a hindrance.

Something snatched Lavida up. It was such a surprise to the woman that she let go of my collar. Her feet lifted from the ground as whoever was on the other side of her used both hands to pick her up. Seconds later, she was tousled across the floor, landing at the base of the steps. Coughing and gagging, I tried to stand, but I didn't have a lot of time before a wrinkled, veiny hand reached down and yanked me to my feet. His skin was hideous, an odd shade of brown and putrid green. I recoiled at his touch but still couldn't make out my savior's face. The blood had smeared across most of my opticals.

"Who are you!" I shrieked as the monster in the white lab coat grabbed my hand, yanking me along the soggy flooring.

"There's no time to explain." The heavy voice barked. "They're waiting for us outside." The rioting all around me became nothing more than background noise as my tense fear began to subside. He didn't look like I remembered, but the voice had become familiar. I knew who it was that had saved me. Straightening my glasses, I tightened my grip on the hideous hand. "Thank you, Raph."

Raphiel was right. It only took a few moments to eyeball the old van with the busted door. The girl at the receptionist's table was sitting comfortably behind the wheel as the tall man who had saved her hung from the passenger's window. His head was popped out of the opening, and even though I couldn't quite make out everyone through the drying blood on my glasses, I would bet money he was smiling.

"What took you two so long?" he called, waving a hand in our direction.

"We saw Sally's car. She made it out right before the prison break... What happened exactly?" Delilah scratched her head as she shifted the van into drive. Slipping into the back, I wrinkled my nose and scooted along the crusty flooring. Raph was right behind me.

"Ugh, it still smells like Quonk in here," I complained.

"In this heat and what you're covered in, I'd be more concerned about smelling like a dead body." Delilah backed out of the parking spot with urgency as the man beside her twisted around in his seat. "I'm Rhudis. Heard you and your friend have been looking for me. I'm not in the business of keeping people waiting, but as you can obviously see, I was otherwise indisposed." Delilah giggled. Taking my glasses off, I used the clean spot on my shirt to wipe them the best I could. It wasn't perfect, but I could at least see who had joined me on this merry adventure.

"You're the girl from the store," I said flatly. I wasn't sure how to take her presence. Had Raphiel been mistaken? Was she not a dangerous Rougarou? Taking a right towards the fairy loading station, Delilah eyeballed me in the rearview mirror.

"I'm Delilah. I'm sure you've heard a lot about me. Don't worry, Smita put a leash on me so I can't kill you... Yet."

"Where is she?" I asked as I turned around, sitting up on my knees.

"She's meeting us at Office 12. That's where you're Wendigo's hiding..." Putting a finger in the air, Delilah booped Rhudis on the shoulder and then giggled again.

"Don't forget, HE'S there too. If Neith has any say, they're going to wake him up and do a little damage." Rhudis didn't have a response to what the girl had announced.

"Shit! I left the box in Office 3. I have no way of securing the Psychopomp."

"I don't think that's going to be an issue. I only saw Peter and Sally get into the car." Delilah replied with a sigh. I didn't like what the woman was saying. It put our original plan to bed... But to be honest, everything had kind of gone up in smoke after Quill let all the monsters loose. Flipping around, I flopped back down on my butt, looking over at Raph. He had curled up against the corner of the van. Hugging his knees, he had pressed his head against them, hiding his face. Something told me to inch closer, so I did.

Reaching out, I touched his wrinkled hand with as much gentleness as I could. The man pulled back a little at first but then relaxed. I could tell that his real skin color was beginning to return.

"How did you do that?" I asked quietly. I didn't want the others to hear. It wasn't their business.

"Rhudis showed me a few tricks earlier. I didn't know how much it would take out of me." Raphiel's breathing was heavy and difficult. His dark hair fell over his pointy ears. Scooting closer, I put my other hand on top of his.

"Well, whatever you did, you saved me. I was cooked before you came along."

"I'm hideous," Raph whispered. "I caught a glimpse of myself in the tile as I was changing."

"No," I responded quickly. "You're my hero." Lifting his head up, the man smiled. Even though his skin was old and wrinkled, and his eyes were murky green, I could still make out Raphiel. He was my friend, and I cared about him no matter what form he took.

"Don't make me vomit!" Delilah said, breaking up the sentimental moment.

"If you'd eat something, you'd be able to control your shifts better. You wouldn't be so spent all the time, and you'd be stronger."

"Stronger than THAT?" I asked in amazement. "He threw a three-hundred-pound mutant across the floor like it was nothing. Any stronger, and he might be able to lift a house." Laughing at my comment, Rhudis shrugged and looked over at Delilah with warmth.

"It helps when you love the person you're trying to save." Raphiel tried to ignore what the man was saying, but I could see his cheeks, which had returned to normal, along with the rest of him beginning to turn cherry red.

"It sounds like the original plan has gone to hell. What are we doing now? I barely talked to Smita on the phone before the doors opened in Office 6." Raph's question was valid; I just didn't have an answer.

"I don't really know," Delilah responded. "The last thing she said to me was to get back to the island before the phone cut out. There was some kind of electric charge. It ran through the whole building. Kinda freaked me out because I have this nasty shock collar inside me. I don't want it to go off again."

"That would be the Raiju. I saw it cut through a guy right before we escaped. It was in its electrical form, probably sucking in all the power it could muster." I replied.

"Don't they usually look like foxes or weasels?" Rhudis asked. "How did you know what it was."

"Trust me, once you've been zapped by one of those things, you don't forget them."

Chapter Twenty-Two
Inside Office 12

Pulling up to the little building surrounded by fencing and double guards at each entrance, Sally and Peter exited the car and walked to the front. Fishing around in her purse, the woman pulled out two security badges and handed one to Peter.

"What are these?" the man asked as he put the lanyard over his head. The little plastic card hung against his black shirt. He decided he didn't like the way it looked but knew Sally wouldn't let him take it off. It wasn't time to be defiant... Not yet, anyway. There was far too much at stake already to reveal who he really was.

The original plan was to escape, simple as that, but between Peter's protests about saving Sasha and the great escape of the others this morning, things had changed. Peter and Muhish wished they had been there long enough to see those sadistic scientists face the monsters they tortured without the safety net of a thick glass barrier. The carnage would have been poetic.

"This is so you can get around the facility. Only people with the right clearance can see Thomas." The two of them walked into the office. Peter managed to look over his shoulder as the door closed softly behind them. He doubted the stupid white plastic that sat around his neck would grant him passage back out. He couldn't help but hope beyond hope that Muhish knew what he was doing. If it were solely up to Peter, he would have run the moment they had gotten to the parking lot.

"Since I've already agreed to do your bidding and were safe from unwanted ears, do you mind me asking what it is you expect to gain from resurrecting Thomas Henderson? He's not exactly controllable. It's impossible to gauge what state he'll return to." Pursing her lips together, Sally frowned as she tightened her grip on the little purse she held in front of her. The wrinkles in her lips were accentuated by the bright red lipstick that had gone on an adventure inside them.

"Mr. Nightingale, I doubt you'll be able to understand the nature of my mission." Sally's pointy shoes tapped along the white flooring. Each step echoed loudly. "When my husband,

Morgan, founded Lupin Corp, we were fresh-faced kids right out of college. He had high hopes for the advancement of medicine. That poor, naïve man wouldn't even consider sharing the company with Nanjoglobe. No, he wanted to branch out independently and make his own advancements. We were going to tank. Lupin Corp was losing money hand over fist. I had to do something… Anything to get my husband's brainchild out of the toilet."

As Peter listened, he knew the woman was talking more to herself than to him. Even after all those years, she was still trying to convince herself that what she had done was right. "I met with Marcus while he was out of town, in Arizona, to be exact. I gave him the serum that he eventually synthesized and used on Thomas. Of course, there were a lot of things to consider back then, like the dumping of Aphiborden runoff, and for a slight fee to keep my husband's tiny business intact and my son in expensive clothes, private schools, and a few houses, I fixed that problem. We opened a fake bread factory, gave away what little product we actually made to the town, and used the lake as a dump site. We even managed to write it all off as a charity. No one would care about a shithole out in the middle of nowhere. Hell, I wouldn't have even known about it if my husband's cornfed family hadn't been raised there."

"You're talking about Holly's Grove, aren't you?" Peter asked. There was no judgment in the man's voice. He was simply stating a fact. Sally nodded.

"I thought the Pheromones would help the ecosystem, not damage it, but I was wrong. The people in town began to change... Mutate even. When those two hikers vanished up on Hollowtail, Morgan didn't know what I was doing. He was always such a do-gooder, even up to his disappearance. When the town tried to sue our company for the chemicals it had been dumping, Nanjoglobe raised our hush money and got us the best lawyers in the world. We were essentially untouchable. I guess that's why I didn't think leaving William with Morgan's nephew, Trevor, would be such a big deal. I know it was a dumb idea. I should have taken him with me, but I had been waiting for two years to merge with Nanjoglobe. Marcus finally gave me the green light, and I wanted it all to work out seamlessly. Nanny Unbarr had an emergency less than eight hours before the big meeting. It was a mess."

"Something happened to William?" Peter asked. Stopping at an elevator, Sally typed in a six-digit code and waited for it to open.

"Unfortunately, yes. Even after I pleaded with Will not to go out to the trail, he managed to escape through an open window and made it down to the infected lake. He mutated and attacked his cousin. Trevor killed him."

"That's horrible," Peter replied without inflection. The doors to the elevator opened, and Sally walked in with Peter right behind her.

"Of course, I took my pound of flesh. I killed the man and his little waitress girlfriend. They wanted to cut Will up and feed him to the locals. I just couldn't have that. Then I heard the crying and discovered Lavita in the kitchen. Well, I shouldn't call what that girl was doing crying, more like croaking. She was so small, and I had just lost my son. I did what any mother would do. I took her." Peter could hear the elevator's gears as they slowly climbed up to the third floor. The doors opened, and another white hall was there to greet them.

"I'm still not sure I follow. What does this have to do with Thomas?" Peter asked.

"Well, that damned Penelope Hillsdale hid Thomas from our company. She stole intellectual property from Nanjoglobe. Of course, Marcus wasn't interested in finding Thomas, and for some reason when I brought up looking for the boy, Marcus forbade it. He was the primary shareholder then, and I couldn't do much about it. About a year ago, his son, Seven, took over. He liquidated all the assets of Nanjoglobe, leaving most of the leftovers to me. Seeing as my husband was a great philanthropist, Seven didn't bother going after Lupin Corp. I'm assuming Mr. Ingrum thought the left hand didn't know what the right hand was doing, so to speak. I wanted to continue my husband's work, and in a way, I have. We've found rejuvenative qualities in vampires' skin for beauty treatments, the blood of Banshees can cure some cancers, and the soft tissue of a Siren's brain may reverse Alzheimer's. I've done all this good in the world; I just want one thing back. This one fucking thing."

Peter stood there in amazement, listening to the woman's story while she typed in her code, pressed her thumb against the pad, and scanned her eye. She couldn't honestly think that this was one simple request... Could she? It took the strength of a meteor to keep Thomas Henderson down for the count.

It was the night of Deanna Loveless's eighteenth birthday, and she was having a pretty big celebration out at the Loveless Estate. Her father was over the moon to have her back. You see, she had been locked away in a mental health facility for the better part of eleven years. After the disappearance of her mother, she had never really been the same. There were some talks of a cult, The Children of The Eternal Inferno, being in attendance that night. Some of the more superstitious people in Eagle's Nest thought that was why the Meteor fell. Obviously, the cult had willed it into being. Other more logical people insisted that the giant flaming ball was simply missed and had been hurtling toward Earth for a while now. Either way, no one lived to tell what happened next... Even Thomas. The Loveless Estate and all that were there were reduced to embers. The only body that hadn't been destroyed was Thomas's. Lupin Corp had been looking for the boy for a while now, and they figured he had been hiding out at the estate... Infatuated with the young woman. Before that, Sally assumed he had simply been living with his adoptive family. There had been a long gap where she wasn't allowed to go looking.

Standing in front of the boy in the blue bubble, Sally and Peter watched him. He was just hanging there. Occasionally, a bubble would pop out from his nose or mouth, but no other movement could be detected.

"You know what they say, don't you?" Peter whispered, but in reality, it wasn't really Peter. The next thing the man said Peter himself had never actually heard. It was something ancient. Something the cult had uncovered, and most dismissed as a fairy tale or lies... Propaganda to keep the masses in check. "They say that this kid is the antichrist. He would be baptized by fire, along with his bride, and then reborn... Blossomed from a cocoon, ready to end what we have started. It's what that cult thought."

"Is that what you think?" Sally asked with a little smile. Peter could tell that the woman wasn't buying what Muhish was selling... Not this time. Peter could feel the Psychopomp inside of him jitter and move. He didn't like the nervousness but kept his cool anyway.

"It doesn't really matter what I believe. Is all of this worth bringing back a child you lost almost twenty years ago? In my experience, they don't always come back the same."

Pursing her lips, the woman dropped her purse down in front of the bubble the boy was in and put her hands on her hips.

"Well, you brought Kasey back, and she's the same annoying woman she was before I poisoned her and Davis sicked that stupid dog of his on her... She the same."

"Not exactly the same," Peter said as he put a finger in the air. "You gamble with a lot of lives here... Especially if Thomas remembers who he really is... And I suppose that's exactly what you're hoping for because if he doesn't, he won't know how to bring back your kid." The anger on Sally's face grew as she looked the man in the eye.

"You didn't have any intentions of bringing him back, did you?" She hissed. "You just wanted a little field trip out of the cell I put you in. Why didn't you just vanish the moment I took you out into the parking lot?" Smiling, Peter shrugged.

"I couldn't let you run free with that nuclear warhead sitting in some goo over here in 12 now, could I? Plus, you still have Sasha and Zanza. Even though I've lost my humanity, I haven't lost my sense of right and wrong. The Elders have been nothing but good to me over the years, and I would like to keep their services for as long as I can." A few bubbles began to form inside the bulb as Thomas's hand twitched a little. "How long has he been doing that?" Peter asked as his concern grew.

"That was the first time... Maybe I don't need you after all."

"How long until we get there?" Kasey asked as she rolled around under the thick wool blanket.

"Not long," Smita said with annoyance. Delilah and the others had met up with Kasey, Smita and Neith back at the hotel room. The sun was still high in the sky, preventing Kasey from going out like a normal person. Wrapped in a blanket, she had made a run for it, leaping into Raphiel's arms. Smita had taken another comforter, the thickest one she could find, along with some industrial tape, and closed off the broken door as best she could. It didn't matter how little the sun peeked through; Kasey continued to cower in the corner behind the others, under the blanket for protection.

"I still don't understand why we couldn't have waited for nightfall. Kasey is virtually useless to us right now."

"That's crap, and you know it, Neith!" Smita declared as she shot the woman a solid stare. "Does the term 'Green Witch' mean anything to you?" Scoffing, Neith rolled her eyes.

"When you say that, I think of a little old lady in her begonia garden. What good is some homemade cough syrup going to do me?"

"That's not all she can do," Smita mumbled. "Were you able to contact Davis?" Nodding, Delilah looked over at Smita and held up her phone.

"He knows what to do. We just have to get there. He said he got an alert on his computer about the cryptid escape… He's not thrilled about how that went down."

"Neither am I," I replied. "I didn't know that little guy could open all the doors."

"What little guy?" Smita asked. "Davis said that Office 3 was empty now that they moved the Psychopomp up to 6." I shrugged my shoulders.

"He might actually believe that. There was this little pink fellow in the cell beside us. I thought he was a prisoner, too, but it turns out he was astral projecting. Smita, this kid wasn't like anyone I've ever met before. I could tell that the travel was messing with his memory, and half the time, he would talk over himself or reminisce about home… But when he was in his element and able to harness his powers he was strong, like scary strong. He created the guards that threw me and Neith in the cell beside him."

"What? No, there was no way those two guards were figments of some kid's imagination. I felt their hands on me. They pushed us into the cell. You have to be mistaken." Neith said in dismay.

"I'm not. I promise. He even changed the environment as he talked to me. I'm assuming it was the prison from where he used to live. I tried to talk some sense into him, but it was useless. That was until I kind of tricked him and asked if he wanted to play hide and seek."

"Is that when he opened all the doors?" Raphiel asked. I nodded, straightening my glasses again.

"He wanted everyone to play. He told me he was going to go hide, and then he just vanished."

"You don't know where he would have gone to?' Rhudis asked.

"No," I replied. "My best guess is that he's back down in the basement talking to himself again."

"Man, if we could get a guy like that on our team, we would be unstoppable," Neith muttered.

"Not the way he is," I spoke. "He's unpredictable."

Delilah turned towards the back of Office 12. I could tell that she held her breath as she did so. I guess it was like holding your breath when you passed by a graveyard. It never hurt to have luck on our side. I could make out Davis standing at the back door, talking to two guards as we pulled up. He looked nervous, but then again, when did he not?

Lifting his head, Davis waved us to the door and then rushed to the back.

"What took you so long? Are these all the monsters you were able to rustle up?"

"Umm... Yes?" Rhudis replied as he eyeballed the man in the white coat. Delilah could tell that Davis was a little more than surprised to see the Rougarou sitting in the passenger seat. As he popped his head through the open window, he looked back at Smita, Neith, and I. Kasey was still hunkered down under the blanket.

"Play nice," Smita whispered. "He's a friendly... Just like you." Biting his lower lip,

Davis swallowed down his better judgment and lifted an eyebrow.

"I will if he will." Davis mouthed back.

"This is a little more important than some vendetta. I'll get back to you in good time." Rhudis purred into the man's ear.

"That's enough of that!" Smita said as she snapped her fingers at the two men. "What's the plan to get us into the Office."

"Follow my lead, and we'll be fine." Pushing Rhudis back into the van a bit, Davis pointed to Raphiel. "I need you two to switch places." Davis looked over his shoulder to make sure the two guards were preoccupied. At this point, they were standing by the door, but they were talking back and forth between themselves, unconcerned with what Davis was doing. "Keep Kasey under the blanket, and for the love of God, don't let them see her face," Neith smirked, blinking her large brown eyes.

"I can keep the guards distracted. Don't you worry, your little head?" The moment Davis looked back at the Siren, his eyes began to glaze over, and he got a dumb smile on his face.

"Stop doing that!" I exclaimed as I slapped Neith on the shoulder. "We're going to need him focused on things other than you right now." Ripping her eyes away from the man, Neith stuck her tongue out at me as the two men in the van switched spots. Blinking a few times, Davis snapped out of the trance Neith had put him in. He tried to act like nothing happened, but everyone in the van knew Neith had him wrapped around her finger.

Taking a deep breath, Davis opened the door and pulled Raphiel from the passenger seat.

"I'm glad you got the new receptionist and the housekeeper out of harm's way. Great job, Mr... Weiner?" Raph tried not to giggle. Instead, he puffed out his chest and tapped a finger against his name tag.

"It's Mr. Winner, sir. It's French." Raphiel could hear the guards laughing quietly where they stood. The engine cut off seconds later, and Delilah popped out of the driver's seat. Sauntering to the back of the van, she pulled the comforter from the opening and grabbed my hand. Neith followed closely behind. Rhudis and Smita hugged Kasey, wrapping her tighter than a burrito as they rolled out from the opening, hoping the guards didn't ask where their chains were.

"Is that all of them?" The first guard asked. "They look pretty flimsy." Looking over at his partner, the second guard slapped him on the back of the head.

"Duh, you idgit. They're the ones that doctor dude was able to wrangle up. The real big nasties probably vanished into the night... Hey, why is that one in a blanket?" Pushing her way through, Neith smiled gleefully and touched the second guard under his chin with her long piano fingers.

"She's scared of the sun. It hurts her eyes." Neith said in her best smoke show voice. Seconds later, both guards giggled like children at recess, stumbling over each other to impress the pretty girl.

"Rob!" The second guard barked as he snapped his fingers. "Why don't you let this lovely lady inside? I'm sure she's tired of standing out here. She's been through quite an ordeal."

"My friends and I don't know how we can repay you." She purred. Flipping her braid off her shoulder, Neith looked down, placing the toe of one shoe over the other. I watched in disbelief as the first guard fought with his key ring.

"I still can't wrap my head around her ability," I whispered. "She looks... Well, she looks kind of ripe from where I'm standing. Why are these men falling over themselves trying to get on her good side?"

"We can see her true form because we've been gifted true sight. A lot of humans don't have it." Rhudis explained.

"I kinda wish I didn't have it," Raphiel replied as he came up beside me. "There's a lot of things I wish I didn't have." I thought back to Office 6 and Raphiel's transformation. I couldn't fathom what he must have gone through to save me. He looked absolutely normal now, but less than thirty minutes earlier, he could have passed for an extra in a zombie movie. If what Rhudis had said was true, and Raph had feelings for me, it must have been even harder to expose his true nature.

Finally, the back door opened, and the second guard bowed as he allowed Neith to walk inside.

"Well?" She asked with a wink, "What are you waiting for? An invitation?"

Chapter Twenty-Three
Transmutation and Other Messed-up Stuff

"You thought you could just waltz in here and take what you want?" Sally screamed as she looked down at Peter. Everyone had exited Office 12, everyone that was except for Sally, Peter, and the last of the Elders. Zanza and Sasha stood chained to the pillars that held the boy in the blue bubble. They both looked battle-worn and exhausted. There were large bits of skin missing from Sasha's once-flawless face. Peter knew that without blood his friend had no way to heal herself.

Sally had gotten the man to his knees, chained in classic cuffs. Beside Peter sat a little golden box with the same sigils that had housed the Psychopomp earlier. He didn't know how she had done it, but the moment she realized she wasn't talking to the Necromancer anymore, she pulled the box from her purse and began to chant. Seconds later, Muhish was inside his golden coffin, and Sally was in full control. It was stupid to think the old lady was nothing more than an old lady. She obviously didn't get to the position of power she was in by being stupid. Peter figured she was closer to death than Sally would have liked, and if she got her son back, she would need a little extra time. Why wouldn't she have memorized the text from the Angel Book? That was if she had somehow acquired it. The last time Peter had heard about it being used was in Crimson Ridge. That had been years ago, and the damage it left behind was nothing short of catastrophic. That just goes to show what putting ultimate power in the wrong hands can do.

"Did you get that trick from the old farmer?" Sally had been pacing the floor with little concern for the monsters around her. The spell that she had cast had made her virtually untouchable by Cryptids.

"I don't understand the question." She sneered as she continued to pace. "Is that an analogy for something?" Peter laughed, but something in his side had begun to hitch.

Muhish had taken more life out of him than he had initially thought. He was far from full power.

"Why don't you let Sasha and Zanza go? They can't help you. Isn't it me you want?" Laughing, Sally finally stopped walking and put her hands on her hips. Tapping her foot, she looked down at the man with a look that said she knew a little more than she was letting on.

"I wanted you to help me, Mr. Nightingale. I wanted that not just for myself but for the world's future. A natural... Or should I say the most natural return I could give him would possibly put the boy at ease... Now we're going to have to do this the hard way."

"What do you mean?' Peter spouted. Looking around the room, he tried to find something he could use, but there was nothing. There wasn't even a living person close enough to siphon energy from.

"Did either of you find it weird that I invited Zanza to the party? You didn't seriously think I wanted the Elders' permission to do something I was going to do anyway... Did you?" The woman laughed again and then rolled her eyes. "Aww, you DID, didn't you?" Her pointy shoes clacked over to Sasha's uncle. They echoed around the room like a swarm of angry hornets.

279

Pressing her wrinkled hand against the man's face, Sally clicked her tongue to the roof of her mouth.

"Let him go! You don't get to touch Zanza Shenea!" Sasha growled as she pulled against her chains. They were made of silver, and the more she pushed, the louder the sizzling sound became.

"You can't use that on me!" Sally yelled. "You two are what's left of the Elders. All the others were hunted down or killed themselves. Living forever is overrated. If it was something I coveted, don't you think I would have taken the midnight kiss a long time ago? Imagine... Me old and wrinkled walking around here for another millennia. Ugh, that sounds horrible. Do you ever wonder if Kasey resents you for making her into a vampire? Especially now, with that pesky blood disease. Her life must be absolutely miserable."

"Actually, it's not so bad," Kasey said from the doorway. Turning around, Sally eyeballed the woman as she let her hand drop to her side.

"You again?" Sally asked as she walked a few steps closer. "I figured you'd be missing the action... Seeing as the sun is out. How'd you get in here anyway?" Looking over the woman's shoulder, She could barely make out Davis's pale face. "TRAITOR!" She screamed through gritted teeth.

"Oh, if you think that's bad, you ain't seen nothing yet!!" Smita called from behind the vampire. Pulling a little yellow syringe from her pocket, she jabbed Kasey in the arm with it, pushing the plunger.

"What was that?" Sally asked as panic began to wash over her face. "WHAT WAS THAT?"

"Just a little something you've been harping on me to perfect. I think it'll do nicely for what's coming." Davis called. He tried his best to join in the taunting despite the fear. He knew it was far too late to switch teams again. This was his way out... One way or another.

Kasey shook a little as her skin darkened. It looked like she was getting an instant tan. Sally paid her no mind. Lifting her hand, she closed her eyes and began to chant.

"I thought you said she was going to go for the skylight," Smita whispered as she eyeballed Davis. The man shrugged a little and frowned.

"That was before I saw Zanza and Sasha. I don't know what the hell she's planning."

"Great..." Smita said with a groan.

As the woman continued to chant, Zanza fell to his knees, coughing and clawing at his eyes.

"What's going on!" He yelped between coughs. Sasha covered her mouth to stifle a scream. Zanza's eyes had disintegrated, and the blood that was once inside his body began to pool around him. It defied gravity, swirling and twirling towards the top of the bubble. Every last drop of life-giving elixir now hovering over the bubble's opening. Letting out another heartbreaking scream, Sasha fell to her knees as well. She wasn't hurt, not physically, anyway. Sasha just couldn't believe that her uncle was gone forever... Leaving her as the last woman standing on the council of elders.

Running towards the woman, Kasey held out her hands, ready to strike. Her eyes flashed from blue to black and back again. Her head felt swimmy, but she had to try. Grabbing the woman from behind, she yanked her down onto the white flooring. All the oxygen left Sally's body in one failed groan. The chanting stopped, and the heaviness in the air began to cease. The laws of physics regained control as the blood that had been hovering over the fishbowl fell into it with a sploosh.

Grabbing Sally's collar, Kasey walked towards Davis with a look of satisfaction.

"So," She began with a grin. "This stuff really gives me immunity?"

"Immunity from what?" Smita asked as she looked over her shoulder to Davis.

"Everything," Davis said with a smirk. "It doesn't last forever. Last time we worked on it, I think its half-life is about an hour."

"No, you don't know what you're doing," Sally said as she instinctively covered her hands with her face.

"Oh, but I think I do," Kasey replied as she retracted her fangs, sinking them deep into Sally's neck. Smita couldn't bear to watch. She hated seeing life leaving someone. It brought her back to her father and what had happened all those years before. The gift she had been given hadn't been worth his life. Grabbing Davis by the shoulder, she looked him in the eye.

"Get out of here. Take Sasha and Neith, but first, have her compel the staff to evacuate, and don't forget to disarm the doors. We might have to make a quick exit."

"What do you mean," Kasey asked as she dropped Sally's now lifeless body to the floor. "We got her. It's over."

"No," I replied as I pointed to the boy who was now moving in the purple water. "I think it's just begun."

"We can't be that far from it. I'm all itchy." I began. Rushing down the hall, I investigated cell after cell. There was nothing in them.

"Maybe you just have fleas," Raphiel replied with a grin. Rhudis also thought that was funny but did his best to hold in his amusement. My right hand held Raph's. I don't think it was a conscious decision; it was just the natural thing to do. The other held an old bone knife. Before the others had gone to the third floor looking for Sally Wells, Davis, and Kasey showed me a room they called the trinket room. It was anything but. Each glass case held the surefire way to kill or at least trap each Cryptid they collected. Even though Kasey hadn't been able to find a way to reverse the curse, she had made me a hex bag filled with powder. She told me, if I needed it, to throw its contents into Wendigo's face. It would loosen its hold on me, hopefully long enough to cut off its head. I could tell that Rhudis and Raphiel were less than happy with the idea. Killing Cryptids wasn't in the job description, but something had to be done.

I stopped, sniffing the air and then pointing to the end of the hall.

"He's around the corner," I said as my eyes flashed a shimmer of bright blue. Raphiel didn't notice, but Rhudis did. He hovered back a little as I pulled Raph along like a puppy on a leash.

"Couldn't we, I don't know, talk to the man... Maybe see if we can convince him to leave."

"No!" I said angrily. "He'll never leave me alone. I'm his now, and that's no way to be... We've got to kill him." I tried not to think about what might be happening above us as we rounded the corner. My teeth began to grow as the hunger in my belly became overwhelming.

"I knew you would return." The Wendigo began. *"Let me out, and we can feast."*

"Dude, that guy's face is funky," Raphiel said as he pulled back my hand. "Birdie, are you sure you can handle this?" My head was down, and I knew my breath was shallow and panicked. I had forgotten how hard it was to control myself when I was so close to the ancient beast.

"I have to try," I muttered. Looking over at Rhudis, Raphiel shrugged. Walking down to the hallway, Rhudis opened the control panel and typed in Davis's code. Seconds later, the door opened, and the Wendigo stepped out. I tightened the grip on Raphiel's hand, trying with all my might not to attack him.

The beast in the ragged clothes touched my cheek and pointed to Rhudis. I could tell he sensed the older Rougarou's power and wanted it for his own.

"*It's time to feast.*" The monster began. I couldn't control it. There was no way to fight; I let go of Raphiel's hand, charging towards Rhudis. Raph attempted to follow, but the Wendigo snatched him up with a bony hand.

"Awe, come on now, Steve! I thought we were cool." Raph said with a moan. "I really don't want to have to do this… Not twice in one day."

Chapter Twenty-Four
The Boy's Return

The glass began to break as Thomas beat on it furiously. Davis and Sasha had barely made it off the third floor and into the elevator before the first drops of purple junk hit the white linoleum. Kasey had pushed the others behind her, watching with concern.

"What are you waiting for?" Peter asked urgently. "break my chains so I can help!"

"Oh, I'm sorry. Was that what you were doing? Helping?" Kasey asked as she wrinkled her nose. "I can't believe you were going to offer your services to the likes of her!" Pointing down to the dead body of Sally Wells, Kasey sneered and then looked back at the man.

"You don't understand. Zanza and I were trying to get Sasha back, and if I managed to get a little humanity along the way, then that was just gravy... You know? Kasey, you've got to believe me. I may not have emotions like you anymore, but I still wouldn't have hurt her. I remember what it was like to love, and Sasha, she's the only reason I haven't taken a long dirt nap." The glass beside Peter began to crack more, sending thick shards sliding across the floor.

"Fine," Kasey said reluctantly. "If you even sneeze wrong, you're next on the menu." Running with all her might, Kasey grabbed the cuffs, breaking the chains that held Peter down. They didn't have time to make it back to the doorway before the bubble popped completely. Thomas, Peter, Kasey, and the dead bodies floated around on the floor like a macabre lazy river for about twenty seconds before the drains in the floor washed it mostly away. Gaining her composure, Kasey got to her feet first, then reached down to help Peter.

"He's out!" Smita screamed as she pointed towards the blonde man behind them. Thomas reminded Kasey of a baby giraffe just getting its footing. His knees trembled, and he shivered from the cold. Thomas's skin was wrinkled and pale, almost void of color completely. Peter figured it was from being in that goo all this time.

"Where am I?" Thomas asked as he looked at his hands in disbelief. "I... I don't remember anything." Blinking his eyes, he rubbed them with the back of his hand.

"This? This is what you've all been so afraid of?" Peter asked with a snort. "He's just a boy." Clasping his hands together, Peter looked Thomas up and down a few times, taking in the vision. He could tell that Thomas had been dressed to impress in a past life. His shirt was burned off completely, but his nicely pressed black tuxedo pants were perfectly tailored, even if they resembled ripped-up shorts now. He was barefoot and frightened... Just the way Peter liked his meals.

"What's going on?" Thomas asked again as he swallowed hard. Smita backed away from the door, waiting for a rerun of what had happened to Sally. Thomas was too timid, too weak to help himself, and the others were convinced he would destroy the world once his memories returned.

"I hate to break it to you, but I fear it's time you go back to where you came from, sir. Your time on this earth is at an end."

"What?" Thomas asked as he looked at the wet duo in front of them. "That doesn't sound right. There are things I need to do here. Big things." Frowning, Peter shook his head.

"No, you've already done those things." He replied. "Let me help you." Reaching out his hand, Peter took a few steps closer.

"Be careful!" Kasey instructed but made no attempt to give the Necromancer any backup. The meds Davis had injected her with might have made her immune to everything, but it hadn't made her stupid.

Touching the boy on the shoulder, Peter closed his eyes and began to chant. It was a chant he had memorized years ago, something he had done a million times. He knew what was about to happen, and yet it didn't.

"I said no!" Thomas bellowed. Grabbing Peter by the collar, Thomas threw the man across the room. He flew through the open doorway, hitting Smita and knocking them both for a loop. The boy's eyes darted back and forth between Kasey and the two, still recovering on the floor. "I'll kill you all." He began to chant. "You can't keep me from her! I'LL KILL YOU ALL!"

Kasey took a fighting stance as the boy charged. She didn't have a chance to retaliate before he lifted her over his head. It was an odd, clumsy-looking dance move that ended with her slammed onto the ground.

"Holy shit!" Smita screamed as she ran towards the fight. "Get your hands off of her."

Thomas's attention was only distracted for a second as he slapped Smita across the face, sending her flying in the opposite direction. Hitting the wall, she slid down to a sitting position. Her eyes fluttered and then closed. Blood smeared the wall where she sat. Kasey feared she was lifeless.

"Peter!" Kasey screamed as she was picked up for a second time. "If you meant what you said, get her and get out!" Nodding, Peter scrambled to his feet. Scooping Smita up, he vanished down the hall and into the elevator. Kasey went down hard a second time. She knew the injection wouldn't last too much longer, and her immunity wouldn't make her bones unbreakable. Struggling against Thomas's grasp, she pulled a small plant from her front pocket and jammed it into his mouth. Stunned, the boy jerked away, yanking it from his esophagus.

"What... What is that?" Scooting back, Kasey sat up with a grin.

"Not my most elegant attack, but one nonetheless. Deadly nightshade. Even a little will kill you."

"Not me!" Thomas replied as he threw the plant onto the ground. "Not anymore." Kasey waited for the poison to kick in, but nothing seemed to be happening. What was that blue stuff Sally dunked him in? Why wouldn't he die?

Roaring like a lion, Thomas took all his strength and lifted her for the last time. Slamming her down onto the hard floor, they both heard something snap and then they were falling. The support beams finally gave way, sending them down to the second floor.

Rubble and flooring fell as the two hit the ground below. Kasey was the first to sit up. She could hear it from around the corner. Raphiel was screaming for help, and Rhudis was pleading for his life. As luck would have it, Thomas had fallen face down. He was stunned, but she knew it was only for a moment. Head reeling, she looked around the room for something to help the boys, and then she saw it. Small and square, shining brightly under what fluorescent lights were left. The sigils engraved on the little box reflected off of Kasey's blue eyes.

Climbing over Thomas, she grabbed the box and ran around the corner as fast as she could. Raphiel had changed into something unspeakable. His long, tendrilled arms wrapped around the Wendigo's neck, making it impossible for the monster to bite him. Further down the hall, against the wall by the control panel, I had pinned Rhudis. He had yet to change, but whatever he said kept me at bay. Closing her eyes, Kasey looked down at the box with fear.

"I don't know how long I've got left with this immunity shot." She whispered. "Could you do me a favor and not kill me?" The box moved a little as the flooring that had been pinning Thomas down began to move. She didn't have a choice. Opening the box, she released the reaper, flinching as its bright white wings took flight.

At first, it flew around the room looking at all the commotion, and then it stopped in front of the Wendigo, perching on its shoulder.

"You've taken many lives," Muhish said as the Wendigo loosened its grip on Raphiel's white coat. "It would be foolish of me not to take yours, but that is not the way of this group." Eyeballing the bone knife I had dropped on the floor, Raphiel ripped away from the Wendigo, shifting back into his old form. He darted around them, snatching it up and putting it into the loop of his pants.

Growling, the Wendigo attempted to snatch at the dove, but Muhish easily evaded its grasp. The reaper's wings fluttered in front of the Wendigo's bone face.

Running towards Rhudis, Raphiel pulled me off of the struggling man. Snatching the hex bag from around my neck, he pulled it off and opened it.

"Throw this in Steve's face! He hates it!" Rhudis did as he was told, blowing all the powder into the eye sockets of the monster. Screaming in anger, the Wendigo stumbled back as Muhish began to collect the lives of the humans it had eaten. One by one, he crossed them over, and with every passing soul, the Wendigo began to shrink. Smaller and smaller it became until it was nothing more than a woman standing in front of them.

"Dude. Steve's a Stephanie." Raphiel began.

"What... What happened?" I asked. Smiling down, Raphiel got off of me and helped me to my feet.

"The Wendigo is all better," Rhudis said in disbelief.

"Please," the woman said as she cowered before them. "Please don't kill me." Taking human form, Muhish stood beside the girl solemnly.

"It is not my place. It is not your time." Turning his attention to Kasey, he smiled, tilting his head ever so slightly. "You, on the other hand, have tricked death more than once."

Before the woman had a chance to respond, a set of hands reached out, pulling her back down the hall.

Rushing to her aid, we watched as Thomas pummeled Kasey into the wall beside the rubble from the third floor. Over and over again, he hit her, and we could hear bones breaking.

"Speaking of cheating death," I said with gusto, "Can't you do to him what you did to... What's your name?" I asked as I looked over at the young woman dressed in rags.

"Steve." She replied.

"I told you!" Raph began, puffing his chest with pride. The Psychopomp sniffed the air and then shook his head.

"There's nothing there to take." He replied with sadness. "The boy was born with no soul. I cannot touch him."

"Well, if you're not going to do something, then I will!" I exclaimed. Reaching into Raph's coat, I pulled out the bone knife, charging forward.

"No!" Rhudis exclaimed. He tried to go after me, but Steve stopped him.

"She will die a noble death. If you stop her, then you may activate her curse." Raphiel looked down at the woman and scowled.

"Then I'm dying too." Rushing out into the hallway, Raphiel watched as I jumped onto Thomas's back, attempting to stop the man from doing any more damage to Kasey. Her eyes had turned black once again, indicating that whatever magic she had been using earlier had worn off. Lifting my arms, I tried to plunge the knife into Thomas's back, but he bucked me off like I weighed nothing. Flying back, I hit Raph, who cushioned my fall. The dagger slid across the floor, stopping at Steve's feet.

"Who are you!" Thomas demanded. "I'll crush you all to dust!" Grabbing a piece of floor tile, Thomas lifted it over his head. Then something happened I never would have guessed.

"It's your turn to hide!" Quill called as he popped up between me and Thomas. "It took you a long time, but you found me!"

"Wh... What?" I stammered.

"Well, actually, SHE did. But she said you wanted help. I must have been really good at hiding if you needed help." Quill pointed over my shoulder. Craning my neck, I could make out Delilah as she waved over to us from the crowd of onlookers. Pressing his lips together, Quill turned around, looked up at the man with the tile over his head, and lifted an eyebrow.

"You're hard to find too. Someone kept you sleeping for far too long." Something in the way the boy spoke to Thomas made the man calm down. Dropping the tile, his chin twitched a little.

"Sleep?" He asked.

"Yup. I couldn't find you because you were sleeping. It isn't polite to wake someone up anyway. Are you ready to go? You've got big things to do. She's waiting."

"You can't keep me away from her," Kasey whispered, repeating the words the man had spoken to her on the third floor.

Quill turned his attention to me once again. There was a look of disappointment on his face.

"Can we play again later? I found the weapon, and Mom's been waiting a long time."

"Sure?" I replied. I could feel Raphiel struggling under my weight a little, but I didn't want to get up... Not until the danger had been neutralized. Grabbing Thomas's hands, the two poofed from the room. It was almost as if they had never been there at all, save for the giant mess left behind.

I got up and grabbed Raphiel's hand before coming to Kasey's aid.

"Where do you think they went?" Rhudis asked as he grabbed Delilah's hand.

"To their next adventure." She replied with a smile.

Chapter Twenty-Five
All Wrapped up in a Little Pink Bow

It looked like everything was working out for the best. Davis was taking over the company, Thomas was nowhere to be found, and even Delilah let go of the notion that Raphiel would run away with her. She had Rhudis back, and that was all she really wanted.

Before they left, I asked the woman where she had found Quill. All she had to say in response was,

'Every Lupin Corp branch has an Office 3.'

Of course, Neith wasn't thrilled that the man of her dreams had slipped through her fingers. Thomas's sudden vanishing act had put her in a bit of a funk. Kasey stepped up to the plate, telling the Siren it was for the best and offering her side missions to offset her depression.

Smita could tell that Kasey was a little bummed herself. She had immunity from everything, and instead of being able to walk in the sun, she had to save her friends from danger. That seemed to be all Kasey ever did, and it didn't seem fair. It had been about a week since everything had gone down. Life had returned to normal… well, normal to us anyway, and Kasey had resumed her garden in the basement, even though she didn't live there anymore. There was no need to hide from the big bad cooperation, not now that it was under new management.

Leaning against the open doorway, Smita knocked a couple of times. Looking up, Kasey smiled as she sprayed her purple sage with a misting bottle.

"Smita! What brings you down here?" I figured you'd be back at Lupin Corp with Birdie and Steve. I know there's a lot we still don't know about what Muhish did to the Wendigo." Nodding, Smita leaned against the wall, crossing one ankle over the other.

"I was there earlier. Neith is having a ball helping out. You have a knack with her, you know. I guess you do, seeing as you two are rooming together now." Laughing, Kasey pointed to the folding chairs lined by the wall. The girls took a seat as they continued their visit.

"Have you heard from the reaper lately?" Smita asked a little more seriously. Kasey shook her head.

"Not really. I think he'll come back when my time is up. The company locked him down for a while, so his backlog is probably extensive."

"Let's hope so," Smita said with a sigh. "Davis wanted me to tell you hello and to give you this." Holding out a little ping box with a bow, Smita cocked her head to one side.

"What is it?" Kasey asked as she took the box. Pulling the bow off, she opened the lid.

"He didn't think it was fair you didn't get to watch the sunrise. Maybe this time you get to do something you want to do."

Peter stood at the base of the Elder's Hall. He had been there for the better part of three days. Sasha had been mourning over her uncle, and Peter hadn't been much help. As much as he had wanted to console her, he couldn't find the words. Compassion doesn't come easy for a man with no feelings.

Turning around, the man watched the sun set over the crumbling cemetery stones. It was a morose and depressing view to most, but to Peter, it was beautiful.

"I thought I might find you here." A small voice called. Looking down, Peter saw the little pink man from before.

"What are you doing? I thought you went home." Peter replied, a little surprised.

"I did." Quill quipped with a smile, "But then I remembered I told Birdie that I'd give her a favor if she helped me find the weapon. I just got back from talking to her and that Raphiel fellow. He's a weird one, that Raph." Peter laughed as he looked out along the hillside. His parents were buried out there somewhere, but it had been so long ago now he couldn't quite remember where. The Necromancer couldn't quite get the thought of Muhish out of his mind. He knew one day the reaper would return, and he wasn't sure if on that day he would be so accommodating. Shaking the thoughts away, Peter looked down at the Mesmer with amusement.

"Well then, don't keep me in suspense. What did she ask for?"

"She said she couldn't imagine a life without love in it. I could tell she's really attached to that weirdo Raph, so that might have had something to do with the favor she wanted."

"She didn't ask for everyone to be in love, did she?" Peter asked as he rolled his eyes.

"No," Quill replied dismissively, "She asked for you to have your humanity back." Faster than the pop of a bubble, Quill was gone. Peter wasn't sure anything had changed, not until he laid eyes on Sasha's beautiful face.

The End

If you like this book, you might like Megan Guilliams other publications available on Amazon.

The Rowanda Saga
Moonlit Star and Untamed Blue
COMING SOON!!
Midnight Whispers, The Rowanda Saga Book 3

The Infernal Kingdom Collection
Inferno
Prince of Embers
COMING SOON!!
Queen of Cinders

The Adventures of Seven Collection
One Stop Monster Shoppe
The Scarlett Library
Showdown in Monster Town

The Twisted Realms Series, published through Dark Moon Rising Publications
The Tale of Two Twisted Sisters
Moondust
COMING SOON!!
The Twisted Star
Whimsies Whispers

The QUESTPHELLOW Trilogy
Valley of Blood
Secrets of Shauna
Sons of Horus

The Graycrest Series
Beyond The Gates of Graycrest
MOURNBEAST

Eaden
The Ascension of Zia
Children of the Abyss

*The Dark and Chilling Tales of
Murdock Monroe*

COMING SOON!!
Below Room 8

amazon.com/author/megan.guilliams.writes.91

Megan Guilliams is an Independent Fiction author who specializes in Urban Fantasy and Horror. She is a Franklin County native who lives in Virginia with her husband and two children. When she's not writing Young Adult and New Adult Fiction she enjoys painting. Filling the walls of her home with colorful lowbrow art and Pop art, Megan enjoys bringing her book's characters to life. As a young child Megan dabbled in short stories, often entertaining her peers. While she doesn't hold any specialized degrees that led her to her writing passion, she currently has over twenty novels published on Amazon and Kindle.

For anyone who's ever felt different, there's a place for you in this world!

Made in the USA
Middletown, DE
23 July 2024